DOC
MISSIO

DOCTOR WHO
MISSION TO MAGNUS

based on the BBC television series by Philip Martin
by arrangement with BBC Books, a division of BBC
Enterprises Ltd

PHILIP MARTIN

A TARGET BOOK
published by
the Paperback Division of,
W H Allen & Co Plc

. A Target Book
Published in 1990
By the Paperback Division of
W H Allen & Co Plc
26 Grand Union Center,
338 Ladbroke Grove London W10 SA11

Printed and bound in Great Britain by
Cox & Wymann Ltd
Reading, Berks.

ISBN 0 426 20347 x

1

'Can't you stop it, Doctor?' Peri asked for the ump-
teenth time. The Doctor shook his head and watched
helplessly as the column before him reared up and
down with increasing force.

The TARDIS, his beloved travelling device, was
out of control, hurtling inexorably towards an
unknown future. It was an erratic machine at the best
of times – its exterior permanently frozen into the
semblance of a 1960s British police box – but now it
seemed finally to have gone haywire. Nothing the
Doctor did to the control console had any effect on its
breakneck plunge through time.

'On and on, as if we're being pulled by something!'
the Doctor said desperately.

Peri shook her head wearily. 'We've been travelling
for days, maybe weeks.'

'Mere units of time, Peri, days, weeks . . .' As well
as an extravagant dress sense, the Doctor's sixth
regeneration had a tendency to irrelevant abstraction,

often driving his pretty young American companion to sulky frustration.

'But what's happening, Doctor?'

'We seem to be being drawn into the future against our will.'

'Well, stop it!'

'I've tried everything.'

'Try it again!'

The Time Lord flicked a switch on the console and to his surprise the column stopped abruptly.

'Doctor . . .'

'Shh . . .!' The Doctor bent urgently over the location dials and frowned, making rapid calculations. Finally he straightened. 'We're centuries off course. Forced into an unknown area of time and space.'

'How can that be?' Peri watched the worry remain on the Doctor's usually cheerful face. For once his flippant response to danger was absent.

'I know of only one circumstance that might allow TARDIS takeover; switch on the scanner, Peri.'

Dutifully, Peri obeyed, then started with fear as the screen cleared to reveal the image of a gloomy looking face with a long nose, the eyes of an angry ferret and wearing a top hat whose brim was encircled with a purple band of cloth once much favoured by Victorian undertakers. The yellow hued skin wrinkled, as thin lips spread into a sneering grimace.

'Greetings, dears, how kind to answer my call so promptly. Do identify yourselves, your TARDIS seems familiar but names never were my strong point.'

Peri waited for the Doctor's reply, her eyes remaining fixed on the strange apparition. When no reply came she turned and saw, to her amazement, the Doctor cowering on his knees at the base of the TARDIS control panel, trembling and sweating with fear.

'Doctor, what are you doing?'

'Shut up, Peri. He mustn't see me!'

'Who . . .?' Peri dropped down beside the terrified Doctor.

'What is it? Why are you shivering?'

'Don't let him see me!'

'Doctor . . .' Peri started, only to be interrupted by a booming laugh from the screen.

'Did I hear "Doctor"? Is it the Doctor I have drawn to me?' The laugh became more strident, forcing the Doctor to thrust his fingers into his ears in panic and close his eyes, as if he were a frightened child.

'I'm not here. I'm not here. I'm not here!' the Doctor chanted as if the words would form a spell that would release him from whatever fear had possessed him.

'Oh, stop it, you big baby!' Peri cried in exasperation and jumped to her feet. 'Who are you?' she demanded of the sinister figure on the screen.

Once again the narrow lips parted into a contemptuous sneer. The voice, deep and mocking, called across the TARDIS control room.

'Doctor! You cowardly snivelling little sneak. Stand up at once!'

With horrified fascination Peri saw her companion haul himself to his feet like a chastened schoolboy.

'Sorry,' the Doctor muttered at the screen.

'Sorry? Sorry was never enough to pardon such a boy. Grovelling! Errant!'

'Sorry, Anzor, sorry even so.'

The cadaverous yellow skull now seemed to dominate every corner of the control room.

'Gather yourself, Doctor.' The voice of Anzor had developed a grating authority. 'Collect your inferior wits. Listen to me. Your TARDIS is to be set into trans-replicator mode instantly.'

'I . . . I . . .' the Doctor began to stutter. Then he cried in fear as Anzor showed a short blue rod with a glowing orange tip.

'Remember this, Doctor?' Anzor's voice dripped with oily menace. 'Must I revive your memory of my galvanizer?'

'Yes, I . . . I . . . mean *no*, Anzor; just doing it. Sorry . . . sorry!' His fingers clawed hurriedly at the combination of switches demanded by Ansor.

Peri stared open-mouthed at the Doctor. She was used to his asperity, but this abject terror was just too much for her. On a sudden impulse she turned the switch that controlled the screen. With a fading roar the image of Anzor disappeared. Horrified, the Doctor turned on her.

'You've done it now, you have . . . it wasn't me, Anzor, honest, it was Peri!' As if to mirror Anzor's rage the TARDIS began to shake and shudder as if pummelled by a meteorite storm. Desperately Peri and the Doctor clung to each other.

'What's happened? Doctor? What did I do?'

'Antagonised Anzor! You're for it you are, Peri, you wait. He'll take his galvanizer to you!'

8

The vibrations became intolerable. The TARDIS seemed about to buckle from the forces being exerted on its structure.

'We're being shaken to pieces!' Peri cried out, holding her hands to her ears.

'That's the trans-replicator mode. Through its use one TARDIS can replace another in space. Useful for repairs or obtaining a replacement immediately.'

'You're letting that undertaker freak swap with us, just like that?'

The Doctor looked away, shifting his gaze uneasily. 'You don't understand. Anzor will have his reasons.'

'This Anzor, who is he?'

'You'll find out,' the Doctor said grimly. As if to emphasize his words the shaking steadied to a low malevolent ripple of constant movement, as if building for one final convulsion.

'Anzor is a Time Lord,' the Doctor added. 'The son of a former council leader. I haven't seen him for aeons. Back in my childhood he used to dominate all our lives.'

'Do you admire him?'

'No. Not admire exactly.'

'Fear then?'

'No. At school, on Gallifrey . . . the class of the fourth millennium. Anzor was the . . . what's the word?'

'School bully?'

'Shush! He might be listening!'

The Doctor's obvious cowardice provoked Peri's fighting spirit. 'Let him!' she said and slammed down the switch to bring back the scanner screen. A dazzling star field appeared. When their sight adjusted to the screen they saw two planets in close proximity to each other. Poised between the two blue and white worlds was a spacecraft floating motionless in space.

'That's Anzor's ship?' Peri pointed.

'His TARDIS? No.' Thoughtfully the Doctor tried the navigational controls. Neither response nor movement could be detected.

'I think Anzor has been trapped in a force field – probably caused by that starship.'

'They dragged us here then?'

'No. Only another Time Lord could do that by activating the distress attraction signal. That's what pulled us through space and time: Anzor's call.'

Peri stared at the Doctor, slowly realizing the implication of his words.

'We're taking his place. Held hostage by that ship. We stay until we can attract another TARDIS. Great! The last one stays for evermore!'

'No. We can't do that. We can't attract another TARDIS. Only Gallifreyan Council ships have that emergency compulsion facility. Anzor must be on a mission. Amazing that: I mean, he used to make me do his navigational homework. Didn't know his vectors from his velocities.'

'A dunce as well as a bully. What a jerk. Why didn't you stand up to him, Doctor?'

'Easy for you. You're a girl.' The Doctor grimaced at a sudden memory. 'Somebody stood up to him – Cheevah, his name was. Anzor sealed him in a block of crystal and dropped him from a great height into the school yard.'

'Very funny.' Peri spoke witheringly.

'We had to pretend it was or get a shock from that orb-stick of his.'

'Doctor, get us out of here. I've heard enough of this Anzor creep!'

The Doctor's face showed his horrified reaction to Peri's incautious words.

'Shush!' he admonished, looking at the screen as if the bully might reappear at any moment. Peri pouted – a sure sign she was at the end of her patience.

'Creep. Creep. Anzor is a creep!'

In an agony of apprehension the Doctor closed his eyes, as if waiting for an invisible blow to fall. When nothing happened Peri nudged him. 'Nothing's up, Doc, relax. Grow up and start thinking about freeing us from limbo.'

With a shake of his shoulders the Doctor tried to thrust away the memories of past terrors and to concentrate on the screen. At first his gaze was unsteady, as if he expected to be confronted again by Anzor; when the star field remained steady before him he began to concentrate fully on the motionless spacecraft.

'I've seen that ship. Somewhere. Long time ago or at least a similar model . . .' Adjusting the scanner to a sharper focus brought an enlarged view of the craft. 'It's survived quite a few flights and battles – look at the repairs . . . scars . . . and the weaponry – they're firing, Peri.'

'Who are they firing at?' said Peri, realizing that

the waves of disturbed vision she was experiencing were due to the distorting effect of power transference.

'I don't know. It must be directed down at the planet below. Some sort of sonic cannon, I think – certainly a massive power bombardment. At least it isn't aimed at us, not yet. We must get clear, Peri, before they turn their firepower upon us.'

'What have I just been saying?' Peri said with exasperation, watching the Doctor fiddling with the controls of the TARDIS without the slightest effect.

'How are we . . .?' she started.

'To escape? That answer will become absolutely obvious . . .' the Doctor paused, a small gleam of his usual high spirits returning.

'. . . as soon as we can think of it.'

2

Sil lay in his water tank and allowed the tall female palace servants to pour water slowly over his small, reptilian body. His green skin glistened as the waters washed over him, giving a momentary coolness to his parched scales. The gentle splash of water, and Sil's contented gurgling, were the only sounds to be heard in the marbled room. Multi-coloured silks hung in swathes from the high domed ceiling, adding to the luxuriance of the place.

Sil's peaceful enjoyment was broken by a metallic wheezing, which echoed around the chamber, though no source could be seen.

'Ah!' Sil cried, then smiled and cackled with delight as the serving women cowered away. An object resembling a gnarled oak tree began to appear within the chamber.

'Do not fear, little ones . . .' Sil hauled himself up onto the sitting ledge of his tank. 'It is only a business acquaintance, come to call!' He laughed his manic laugh once more as the blasted oak progressed through the final stages of its manifestation.

Up above the temperate world of Magnus the Doctor's TARDIS remained caught in the web of the force field projected by the mysterious spacecraft. Inside the marooned TARDIS the Doctor and Peri faced each other.

'Let me get this straight, Doctor, we are now where what's-his name, Anzor, was?'

'Anzor is free of the force field emanating from that warship. "Warship", why did I say that?'

'I don't know. Concentrate, Doctor, don't you understand how serious being stuck here is?'

The Doctor shrugged, his thoughts seemingly elsewhere.

'There should be a way . . .'

'Find it then!' Peri urged.

The Doctor concentrated his thoughts, his blue eyes brightening with the effort of finding a solution. After a minute he slumped and shook his head. 'No answer that I can see. What a pity.'

'Doctor!' Peri stormed. 'That undertaker has scrambled your wits. Don't give up: think. Think! Where would Anzor go?'

The Doctor considered. 'Anywhere. Any place or time in the universe, but most probably to that blue planet. Yes, that's the most likely, if he's on a council mission, that's where he'd go.'

'Any chance he might deign to rescue us?'

The Doctor shook his head decisively.

'Oh, no. That isn't Anzor's style at all. He won't care if we're marooned for evermore.'

The blasted gnarled tree trunk completed its appearance, its branches clawing towards the pink dome of the palace ceiling. Sil, carried by the women attendants, came to rest before what he hoped would be the entrance to the object. A panel opened silently and a tall, sombrely dressed figure stepped from inside the tree, doffing his top hat so that its purple band could swirl impressively.

'My dear!' Sil cried, 'It's been ages. Thoros Beta, wasn't it?'

'Probably,' Anzor said non-committally, his eyes taking in the opulent furnishings of Sil's apartment with faint disapproval of such ostentation.

'I've been waiting many days for your arrival, my dear Anzor.'

'Got caught in a force field thrown out by that spaceship of yours.'

Sil held up his clawlike hands in protest.

'Mine? Not mine. I own no craft. You look upon a mere castaway, a humble agent of Amorb. Anzor, you look upon a creature who needs success as much as his skin wants water.' Sil gasped for effect and motioned for his maidens to splash his person. Dutifully each began to take turns at ladling the cooling swampwater over him. 'Ah, Anzor, it is so excessively temperate here.'

'You mean hot. Yes, I suppose it is.' Anzor ran his forefinger inside the collar of his white shirt, then fussily arranged the folds of his black silk cravat. Sil's lips pouted. His ivy green tongue flicked out to moisten his lips before continuing his complaint.

'I must remain simmering here until I can create a fortune that will reinstate me in the respect of Lord Kiv, the ruler of my home planet. Still, now you are here that might become more than a possibility.'

'I am on Time Lord Council business. I'm told you are my contact. So tell me what is happening on this world of Magnus?'

'All in good time.' Sil was too wily a campaigner to allow information to be given away too soon. 'Let us make you comfortable. Refresh yourself; then we will talk. I assure you, Anzor, this planet has many surprises to impart.'

Sil signed to the tawny skinned servants to cease bathing him and to attend to Anzor. Dutifully they led the sombre Time Lord towards a fountain of refreshment that was gently bubbling in a corner of the marbled room.

Aboard the Doctor's TARDIS Peri was staring at the image on the scanner. The Doctor, still oppressed by his encounter with Anzor, stood listlessly beside her.

'Why is that ship forcing so much power down to that world below?' Peri asked.

'I don't know,' the Doctor said and sighed.

'I wonder . . .' Peri started.

'What do you wonder?'

'I wonder why I ever consented to travel with you . . . or not travel in this case.' Suddenly a transformation came over the Doctor.

'Just a moment!' The Doctor pushed the amazed

Peri aside and began to activate the power boost auxiliary system that linked to the energy faculty of the TARDIS. The column moved! Simultaneously the screen showed the mysterious starship moving ever closer to them as the TARDIS shifted its position in space.

'Peri, they have been transferring so much power, they have weakened their hold on us!' the Doctor said excitedly.

'But Doctor, we're drawing closer to them by the second and that cannon is turning towards us!'

'Hold on,' the Doctor yelled as the hexagonal bore of the sonic cannon centred on them. Peri saw a jagged purple flash jet towards them as the Doctor performed a desperate manipulation on the control panel. Peri, braced for the shattering impact of sonic bombardment, was thrown instead into the disorientation of TARDIS time transference.

'Done it! Just enough power left to break clear into a quick dematerialization, Peri. Rather cleverly done, don't you think?' The Doctor flicked a speck of cosmic dust from the sleeve of his multi-coloured coat and beamed at his companion.

'Depends on where we find ourselves,' she replied.

'Not far forward or back: maybe out in space or on that blue planet.' The Doctor paused to check his era co-ordinates.

'Midway through, yes, the twenty-third century, your time, Peri.'

'Not the last decade of the twentieth century?'

'No. Sorry.'

* * *

The underground caves of the Magnii were shrouded in their usual dull light, barely illuminating the group of six male youths who sat cross-legged in the circle necessary for the practice of mind lock. The quavering eerie music produced by their trance echoed from the damp walls of the cavern then was overwhelmed by the more insistent sound of TARDIS materialization. One by one the boys opened their eyes then scrambled to their feet, their mood becoming more and more excited as they watched the outline of the blue police box become clearer. Vion, the leader of the group, lifted an exultant arm. 'At last,' he cried. 'Hold, brothers, hold until our conjuration is complete.' With a great effort to contain their excitement the boys closed ranks, sat down and tried to maintain what they believed was an apparition brought about by their psychic powers.

When the Doctor and Peri came from out of the TARDIS they found themselves facing a group of drably dressed youngsters sitting, arms linked, eyes closed and in a state of trance.

Peri looked sideways at the Doctor who raised a finger to his lips and waited for the boys to realize their presence. After what seemed an age to Peri one of the boys opened his eyes and with a gulp of excitement bade the others do the same. None of the youths spoke. Remaining on their knees they bowed reverently to the Doctor. Startled, Peri nudged her companion.

'What's . . .?' she began. The Doctor grinned.

'About time I received a fitting welcome, don't you think?'

'Nonsense!' Peri addressed the worshipping group before them. 'Stand up, we're not gods or anything . . .'

'Speak for yourself, Peri . . .' the Doctor started to joke, but was interrupted by a boy seizing his hand and kissing it repeatedly.

'Master.'

'Mother,' said two others, each taking one of Peri's hands.

'Hey!' Peri protested.

'Mother?' The Doctor smiled.

'What's going on?' Peri demanded, trying to shake her hands free.

The leader of the boys stepped forward humbly. 'We have tried so long; so many times have we stolen away, met to try and create your presence. Now, when hope had almost died you come in all your majesty and glory.'

The Doctor looked behind him as if Vion might have been talking about someone else. He saw no one, then realized he was expected to reply. 'Why . . . er, thank you, er, you are?'

'Vion. Leader elect of the Magnii.' He indicated the others.

'Just who do you think we are, Vion?' Peri asked quietly.

'Why, the holder of the revelations.'

'What revelations?' Peri blurted out.

Vion looked crestfallen. 'Please, mother, do not pretend, not when we have risked our lives in daring to bring you forth.'

'No. Peri, no pretence, please.' The Doctor turned

Peri aside and whispered in passing. 'Let's find out what these revelations are supposed to be, yes?' Peri nodded, then noticed a flash of light bobbing down a distant passage. Vion also saw the light and its approach galvanized him into urgent activity.

'Come!' he said intensely, grabbed Peri by the arm and pushed her towards another exit from the cave.

'Here we go again,' thought Peri, but allowed herself to be bustled into a gloomy passageway just wide enough to allow the group of boys, herself and the Doctor to hurry away into the enclosing darkness.

After a few seconds a middle-aged woman, wearing a white uniform trimmed with blue edging, entered the cavern. Shining her torch around it was several moments before she discovered the TARDIS.

With a cry of fear the nurse retreated hastily back into the labyrinth of caves that honeycombed the underworld of the blue planet know as Magnus Epsilon.

3

Sil and Anzor had settled opposite each other in the apartment of the palace of Zandusia designated for the use of visiting delegates. Anzor sipped his wine, fiddled with his galvanizer and considered the babble of plans and wildly eccentric ambitions with which the Thoros Betan had bored him for what seemed at least an hour. Finally he lost patience. 'Your plans for buying up the universe don't concern me, Sil. To me you are nothing more than a money-grubbing little slug!'

Sil preened himself, then gave a little bob of appreciation. 'Why thank you for that compliment. Yes, one does need allies here on Magnus . . .' The little green slug-like creature cackled at some obscure memory then continued. 'It's a very strange world, indeed, dangerous especially for males of the human species . . .'

Anzor's gloomy features assumed a scowl of distaste. 'I am a Time Lord. Human? Perish the thought!'

Sil held up an apologetic hand.

'Then you might be all right . . .'

Sil stopped in mid-sentence as the door to his room opened. A woman entered, tall and imperious, wearing an emerald green sari of almost transparent silk. At once Sil became his most ingratiating self.

'My Mistress Rana! How quickly you responded to my humble call!'

The Rana's grey oval eyes ignored Sil and rested upon Anzor. 'You are late, Time Lord.' Her voice was even but with a certainty of tone that signified the confidence of unchallenged authority.

Anzor was unimpressed. 'I am here now,' he said insolently then looked beyond the Rana to where other women dressed in similar fashion had entered.

A ripple of consternation ran through this group at Anzor's contempt but the queenly Rana seemed content to administer only a mild reprimand. 'You address me as Rana Zandusia. I am the elected leader of the seven sisterhoods of Magnus. You will treat me with deference or your stay will be an extremely short one.'

'Are there no men with whom I can deal?' Anzor asked the Rana, the question abrupt, his tone haughty.

'No. A few cower underground. On this world only the female prospers.'

Sil, upset at being ignored in all this, interjected. 'A virus that kills, something they term hormonic. Only women and aliens survive, the great Morgo be thanked for that!' Sil laughed, a burst of discordance that disappeared into his throat like muddy water down a drain.

Anzor shook his head. 'I have never heard of such a world before . . . a virus, you say?'

A slim young woman with large brown eyes and dark hair flowing down to her waist stepped forward proudly. 'We are descended from a colonizing unit that came from third earth. This world of Magnus must have seemed ideal to our ancestors until, one by one, the men sickened and died.'

A slight smile played across the generous mouth of Rana Zandusia.

'Leaving the women to rule.'

Anzor looked at the woman facing him for a long moment before, with a shrug of his shoulders, indicating that it was no great matter to him what gender ruled the planet. 'You have applied to the Council of Gallifrey for permission to incorporate elements of time travel into defensive weaponry – why?'

'We believe a neighbouring planet in our system, Salvak, has discovered an antidote to our atmospheric viral defences against male invasion. We wish to travel back in time, invade Salvak and abort their laboratory research.'

Anzor smiled mockingly. 'We or I?'

Zandusia regarded him coolly. 'We would prefer that you act to protect us.'

'I – a mere male?'

'They have their place. However, the reason we are so advanced technologically is because we women do not see the point of diverting our creative energies into war. But I must say that if we have to go to war against Salvak, we will.'

Anzor shook his head with some enjoyment. 'Request denied. There can be no exceptions for any world. It is forbidden to alter history. My job is to prevent time tampering, to forbid time subversion – not participate in it.'

The Rana frowned. 'That is your decision?'

'Yes.'

'Irrevocable?'

Anzor did not bother to reply. Rana Zandusia motioned to the slight figure of Jarmaya at her side. The young woman began to uncover the stone of a large ring on her right hand.

'I ask you again, Anzor. Help us,' the Rana said.

'You are wasting my time, Madam,' Anzor replied.

'Very well. Jarmaya!'

At the sound of her name, the girl turned the back of her hand away from her and closed her eyes briefly. The gemstone glowed and light burst forth in a brilliant yellow beam that transfixed Anzor, instantly freezing him in a field of arrested energy.

Sil laughed with delight. 'I predicted he would refuse, did I not, Rana?'

'Yes. Now we have his time machine and we have him. We are grateful for your advice, Sil.'

Sil clutched at his forehead. 'But how will you open it. Those TARDIS things are devilish to penetrate.'

Rana Zandusia did not reply at once but walked around the petrified statue of Anzor caught in mid-gesture. 'Simple entry into brain memory. We link his brain, if we can find such a minor object, to a memory osmosynthesis subject so she can pick up his memory recall. It is not easy, but it is possible. That is why we have so little crime on Magnus – because guilt can always be easily established.'

Sil did not like the sound of such a process of memory investigation. 'I would not like to have my memory investigated,' he said in a voice tinged with some alarm.

Zandusia smiled knowingly. 'Then remain our ally and confidant, Sil.'

'Oh, I will, your Ranaship, I will,' Sil replied with all the sincerity he could muster.

The Doctor and Peri groped their way after the small group of boys led by Vion. The sound of an underground spring grew louder. Peri thought of drinking sweet water from a cool stream on a bright summer day; the prospect of such a treat seemed a long way away. All she could think about now was to take one step at a time and to wonder what strange alien world they had found themselves stranded on this time.

'Whoops!' Peri had cannoned into the Doctor, who had halted at a sign from Vion. 'Sorry, Doctor, it's so dark.'

'Yes.' The Doctor turned his attention to the boys who now clustered about them. 'Why do you children live down here in darkness?'

Everyone turned towards Vion, who seemed their spokesman and leader.

'We have no choice,' Vion replied. 'The air on the surface is deadly to us once it mixes with sunlight.'

'Yes,' a smaller boy chipped in, 'A boy called

Gimri, mad Gimri, went upsides and he turned blue, shrivelled up, horrible it was.'

'That's what they said.' Vion interrupted.

'The matrons showed his body.'

'Listen, Asam, just because you're scared . . .'

'Just don't expect me to go up there – that's all!' Asam said, his voice rising with fear at the prospect.

'Keep your voice down, listen . . .' Vion paused, listening to the sound of distant voices 'Someone's coming.'

A tremor of alarm ran through the group. 'The matrons – they've missed us!' Asam turned accusingly on Vion. 'You wait. We'll be down for the long sleep!'

'Oh, stop whining!' Vion pushed Asam and the others to a cleft in the rocks. Fearfully the half dozen boys huddled down with the Doctor and Peri joining them. The erratic light from advancing torches danced and flashed across the dank cavern. The tension became too much for Asam; a choking cry came from his throat. Swiftly Vion clamped a hand across the mouth of the frightened youth, trying to stifle any further outcry. The two boys struggled silently as the lights advanced towards them.

The Doctor stepped out from their hiding place. 'Stay there, all of you,' he ordered and strolled casually towards certain discovery.

The flashlights were held by two white-uniformed women. Taken aback by the appearance of the Doctor the two matrons halted in shocked surprise.

'Who . . .?' the older matron started.

'Yes?' the Doctor replied amiably.

'Was that you crying?' the younger woman asked.

'Yes. Always was a blubberer, can't stand the dark, you know.'

'Who are you?'

'A visitor.'

'From Salvak?'

'What's that?'

The two matrons glanced at each other.

'There was a rumour of a landing . . .'

With mounting interest the Doctor watched the young matron uncover a large yellow ring with a green stone. A shimmer of sallow light escaped from the ring.

'Kill?' the nurse asked her companion.

'No. Just to transfix him will be enough.'

'Just a moment!' The Doctor yelled as a ghastly yellow light shone from the ringstone and enveloped him. In less than a second the Doctor was held frozen in his gesture of appeal, an instant statue in the centre of the murky passage.

'What was the setting?' the older matron asked of her junior.

'A little in excess of sib-stun. Enough to last until the examiners can decide what to do with him.'

Both women shone their lights on the Doctor, fascinated by the strange red coat with its patches of different materials. 'Strange, seeing a man so mature.'

'Yes,' the elder woman said. 'Well past the twenty years usually allowed. I've never witnessed a male so mature, have you?'

'No.' The young woman shut off her torch. 'And I don't want to see one again.'

'Nor do I. Let's get him off to the report station before the enforfreeze effect fades.'

With much effort each woman lifted one of the Doctor's elbows and managed to carry him away.

After a few moments Peri and the boys crawled out into the passage. Peri realized she had been lying in a pool of water and that the clammy feeling was not only through the shock of what she had just witnessed but was also related to the feel of her sodden clothes.

'Do you have to live in such a dump? I'm absolutely soaking!'

'Lots of water underground now,' Vion said. 'It's part of the changes.'

'What changes?' Peri asked crossly.

Vion shrugged. 'The changes that go before the revelations. Surely you know that.'

Peri decided this was hardly the time to reveal that she had not the faintest idea what Vion was talking about. She opted to look wise and act decisively.

'We must follow the Doctor. Save him. Unfreeze him, or something.'

'He's as good as dead,' Asam said gloomily. 'Blue and as shrivelled as mad Gimri.'

'Be quiet!' Peri ordered. To her surprise the boys became quiet and seemed resigned to following her orders. With some amazement Peri realized that her rôle had changed. She was, for once, of the dominant sex. Here males were quite used to finding themselves occupying a secondary rôle. 'Right, let's go. Where is this report station?'

'We don't know . . .' Asam started, but was interrupted by Vion.

'I do. If it is still night up on the surface, I will guide you to it.'

'No. No. No!' the boys exclaimed in unison, whimpering like puppies separated from their mother.

'Shut up!' Vion ordered angrily. 'All of you. Follow me. You too, Peri!'

Well, thought Peri, *my dominant role sure lasted a long time*, but as Vion was obviously intent on becoming a leader set to dare the unknown, she hadn't the heart to object.

'OK,' she said. 'Lead on, Vion.'

The line of boys and the slight figure of the girl began to file along the passageway that would lead them towards the forbidden world above.

4

In the Examining Centre the medium, Ulema, trembled with the effort of linking in to Anzor's psyche. A crowd of interested onlookers waited for a sign that Ulema had made contact with the mind of the time traveller. Ulema's lips moved and formed words that were obviously not from her thoughts but Anzor's.

'Counter thrust, turn, galvanize . . . Up, return to Gallifrey, Vector Matrix, Matrix seven over five . . .!'

'She has made contact,' Zandusia said with approval to Jarmaya, the chief examining officer.

'Let us hope so.' Jarmaya leaned forward to whisper to the medium. 'Be specific: we need the secrets of time travel – it is imperative!'

Ulema's eyelids fluttered but nothing further emerged, although on her smooth young forehead a slight frown appeared as her concentration deepened. Jarmaya glanced apologetically at Rana Zandusia.

'It is not simple. Alien minds are never easy.'

'Yes.' Both women looked from the delicate features

of the medium to Anzor's ugly, saturnine face. Then
Zandusia started with excitement as Anzor's words
began to tumble from the mouth of the medium.

'Seven, six . . . zed-ess. Equal, EQ squared twice.
Rotor operating time CDE. No time specificate . . .'

Jarmaya turned to Zandusia. 'A little more information extracted from this fool's mind could give you
power to become mistress of space and time. Should
you wish to.'

Zandusia considered the thought, a slight smile
hovering on her wide, full mouth. Then more of
Anzor's words began to spill from Ulema's lips and
the Rana turned her attention back to the immediate
problem of finding a means of protecting the future of
her planet.

'Go carefully through that opening and you might get
back into the dorm unseen.'

The boys peered into the darkness indicated by
Vion's pointing finger. Asam hesitated.

'What if the other matrons have missed us and are
waiting. What if they notice you are absent?'

'They won't. Not if you cover for me.'

'What if the sun comes up early, Vion. You'll be
sunsick. Dead,' Asam continued.

Vion spoke scornfully. 'What if Magnus breaks
open and swallows us up? "What if, what if," you
paralyse me with the boredom of your "what ifs"!'

Uneasily Asam moved away. 'You're acting like the
worst sort of regressor, a mad male.'

Before Vion could reply Peri intervened. 'Just show

31

me where I can find the Doctor, Vion, that's all you need do.'

'I said I'd take you and I will.'

'Not at the risk of your life.'

'I'd dare anything if it led to something not found on Magnus.'

'What's that?' Peri asked, puzzled by the light of excitement now alive in Vion's eyes.

'Excitement. Adventure. Conflict!'

Asam and the other boys hurriedly backed away from Vion's words as if fleeing from a curse. Soon they were lost in the darkness leaving Peri and Vion alone.

'Come on, Peri,' Vion said simply. 'Let's go upsides.'

'Stupid machine!' Ulema's voice transmitting Anzor's memory sounded loudly inside the chamber of examination. 'Give it a big kick. Shake it free . . . won't work, it won't work!' The voice became tinged with panic. 'Force field. Why? Who? Try the replicator mode. Yes, get some passing Time Lord to sort it out . . . the Council can't blame me if this piece of junk won't work. Somebody will pay for this. I'm going to do . . . do . . . what . . . what . . .?'

The words trailed away. Perspiration glistened on the skin of Ulema. Her eyelids trembled then opened. She stared dully at the examiners. 'That is all,' she said in a dull flat voice. 'His intellectual capacity is not great. His technical expertise is limited, his mechanical aptitude is less than average.'

Jarmaya bent to Ulema, helping the exhausted girl to raise herself from the couch.

'Enough, sister, it is a start. You have done well.' The Chief Officer's words were interrupted as the two matrons dragged in the still immobile figure of the Doctor. Breathless from their exertions they made their report.

'Rana, we found this invader. We wondered whether he might be from Salvak.' Zandusia examined the Doctor closely.

'That is no Salvakian.'

'Another time traveller?' Jarmaya suggested.

'Why would the Council send two? There is a way to find out . . .' Zandusia indicated the medium Ulema.

'She is exhausted, Rana.'

'I'm sure she isn't.' Zandusia's voice was firm. Ulema smiled wanly.

'I will try, Rana.' The medium watched dully as the Doctor, still frozen into stillness, was placed alongside her.

Ulema closed her eyes, lay back, frowned, her eyelids flickered as if in the realm of dream. She shifted uneasily. Her eyes opened. She glanced first at the immobile Doctor on one side of her then at Anzor on the other.

'Begin,' Zandusia ordered impatiently.

'I am ready, Rana,' Ulema answered dutifully, then closed her eyes in concentration.

Zandusia watched the medium as she lay back between the two unconscious Time Lords. The Rana sensed that unlocking their secrets was vital to the interests of all the women who populated the planet of Magnus Epsilon.

'We must find the key to time travel,' she urged her companions who waited silently, observing the attempt at mind probe. 'Our future depends on it!'

The narrow passageway with its unevenly hewn steps led up towards the surface. Peri could feel the air wafting down. To her surprise it seemed warm, aromatic like a tropical island.

Vion, on a step above her, halted. 'Best you go first from here, Peri. Check all is well.'

The girl climbed past him, sweeping aside the fronds of vegetation that hung down into the chute, and emerged onto a flat grassy plain with a heaven of stars gleaming above in a dark blue sky.

'How is it?' Vion's voice asked anxiously from below.

'Black as a night should be,' Peri called down.

'No sun?'

'Not a glimmer.'

Vion joined her putting a brave face on his anxiety. He stood on the surface that had always been forbidden to him, peering into the darkness.

'I will lead, Peri,' he said in a surprisingly manful tone of voice.

Peri shrugged. 'OK Vion, just as you like. I'm quite used to being bossed about by the Doctor.'

Vion stepped past her then pointed at a cluster of lights in the distance. 'Come on!'

* * *

'Is she all right?' Zandusia asked as all present watched the medium's struggle to make mental contact with the Doctor.

'Eeny-meeny-miny-mo!' Ulema suddenly blurted out. 'Anzor's TARDIS has to go! But if it does, who will know?'

'What is this nonsense?' Zandusia demanded. 'What has this to do with anything?'

'She is tired. I can feel her exhaustion,' Jarmaya said.

'She must persevere!'

A chuckle gurgled within Ulema then spilled out in a tinkle of delighted laughter.

'Why is she laughing?' the Rana asked with irritation.

'Wait . . .' Jarmaya replied, watching the medium intently.

Ulema began to speak lightly and with a definite pattern to her speech that was markedly different from her own. 'Do you like it in here? I can feel you tip-toeing through my brain cells. Tickle-tickle. May I join you?'

As if in reply Ulema giggled with enjoyment at the thought.

'Stop this!' the Rana demanded.

'Please . . .' Jarmaya pleaded as Ulema began to speak once more.

'The TARDIS. That old thing. Simple principle, really. Bit like a water ice on a hotplate . . . oh, no, image only. You want facts or a formula? Well, given that matter expands to a ratio of . . . ah, I see what's happening. I wonder if the technique can be reversed?'

The body of the girl suddenly slumped. The pattern of her speech reverted to what the other examiners recognised as being her own. 'So tired . . .' Ulema said dully. 'Zandusia, planet over-Mother . . . why does she want more, more, more! Ambition to be absolute Queen of us all. Power.'

'Stop this,' Zandusia ordered. 'She is being manipulated by the mind of this fiend!'

'Fiend? What has she been doing to me? Me, the poor old lovable Doctor who only wants to enjoy what looks to be a very pleasant world.'

Jarmaya stared down at the Doctor.

'He's awake, revived, he must be aware of what has been happening to him.'

The steel blue eyes of the Doctor opened and twinkled mischievously up at her.

'You've guessed. Congratulations.'

As if still linked to the Doctor, Ulema's eyes also fluttered open. 'I . . . I lost contact. I'm sorry, shall I try again?'

'No.' Zandusia pointed at the unconscious body of Anzor. 'We may have enough information to obtain access to his time ship. Revive him!'

'Oh, must we?' the Doctor said in mild protest. 'It's been so quiet and restful up to now.'

Zandusia stared coolly at the Doctor. 'I have noted your insolence. Bring both Time Lords to me in my throne room in one hour.' Then she turned and walked regally out of the room, leaving the Doctor to observe the process of arousing Anzor from the effects

36

of the enforfreeze. The Doctor's expression showed some apprehension as a stimulus pad was activated on Anzor's temple, bringing a sluggish response from the sleeping bully.

Ulema eased herself to her feet and walked unsteadily towards Jarmaya. 'He . . . the Doctor he calls himself, manipulated my mind . . . what did I say?'

'Only a tiny joke. I aplogize.' The Doctor smiled at the weary young woman. 'Though what you expressed would be what your mind truly believes. What you said about the Rana is what you really think.'

'What did I say?' Ulema asked in bewilderment.

'She's eager for power,' the Doctor answered before Jarmaya could intervene to halt the exchange.

'No!' Jarmaya protested. 'The Rana is elected. She only wields power because some woman must.'

'The urge to rule can become compulsive,' the Doctor said flatly.

Jarmaya opened her mouth to speak, but her reply was interrupted by a deep groan from Anzor, who had begun to surface from the depths of his paralysis.

'Look at him,' the Doctor said. 'Anzor loves power like boys love breakfast.'

Ulema touched the Doctor's sleeve. 'I must have been very tired to allow a man to best me.'

'We all have our off days.'

'That must be it.'

'Doctor!' the voice of Anzor roared out menacingly. 'You are responsible for this effrontery to my person. Where is my galvanizer stick?'

At the sound of the hated voice the Doctor's poise began to desert him. Lurching to his feet Anzor began to advance on the retreating Doctor. Alarmed at the threat Jarmaya hastily fired a warning beam from her ring. As it penetrated Anzor's cadaverous hide he roared with pain.

'Ow! Who did that? You, madam?' Anzor made to raise a hand in retaliation.

Quickly the Doctor intervened. 'Don't upset these ladies, Anzor. They have access to power and knowledge I don't yet understand.'

'You coward, Doctor. You may be ready to buckle and break, but I'm not going to kowtow to a lot of women . . . ow, that hurt . . . ow!'

Jarmaya turned the glowing ring on her index finger once more towards Anzor who promptly backed away. 'All right, madam, you have made your point.'

'Now will you both act like responsible Time Lords and make yourself ready for an audience with Rana Zandusia?'

Both Time Lords shambled towards the doorway, reaching the exit simultaneously. A struggle ensued as both tried to get through the door at the same time. Jarmaya had to intervene in order to separate the warring pair.

'How childish these Time Lords are,' she observed as she shepherded them into the corridor that connected the examining centre with the inner palace of the Rana Zandusia.

5

Vion and Peri had walked through the darkness towards the palace of light with its satellite dwellings where servants and lesser officials were housed.

Vion indicated the main entrance to the courtyard that seemed to be unguarded. 'Through there.' Peri saw the boy hesitate and glance towards the horizon.

'Shouldn't you be leaving now?' she asked gently.

'I'll see you into there if you want.' Vion indicated the palace. 'If that's where you want to go . . .'

'Will that be where the Doctor will have been taken?'

'Most probably. I've heard the matrons talk about the sisters of science – they work at something called a brain intersection centre.'

'That sounds fun. Let's go . . .' Peri walked towards the entrance of the marble palace that seemed to her to resemble the grand palaces depicted in old fairy tales, with soaring towers and domes that contained . . . what? *Only one way to find out*, Peri told herself as she and Vion went through the open gate and entered the imposing edifice in which she hoped to find the Doctor.

The ancient oak that was the exterior of Anzor's TARDIS resisted the initial attempts at entry, but when Jarmaya's ring was unsheathed and pointed at the bully he agreed to open up without any further fuss. The examiner group entered the TARDIS and found a control room made untidy by discarded items of sombre clothing. Zandusia went to the panel that housed the TARDIS controls. Her gaze was one of intense excitement. Turning to Jarmaya she said: 'Imagine what time travel would mean to us. Imagine the power for good it would give.'

'Yes, Rana.'

'The two Time Lords, they must show us the means of time travel.'

Jarmaya signed to an attendant to have Anzor and the Doctor brought in.

'They will show us, Rana, one way or another,' said Jarmaya, turning the ring of power on her finger to the position of readiness.

The corridor of the palace in which Peri and Vion found themselves was plushly decorated. Rich carpeting felt soft and luxurious beneath their feet, and the walls were hung with tapestries decorated with emblems of wealth and nobility. The atmosphere seemed calm and peaceful – as if the palace had an identity of its own that was confident of its ability to absorb, then repel any intruders.

The muted sound of voices approaching around a corner made Peri pause. Urgently she whispered to Vion, 'I'll shadow whoever is approaching. You must get back underground while there is still time.'

'I don't want to leave you,' Vion said bravely.

'Scram! I don't want it on my conscience if you get caught by the sunrise.'

'You'll be all right?'

'Sure I will.'

'Yes. I keep forgetting you're a girl.'

Peri pushed him away, then realized that they had delayed too long. Two attendants in yellow robes rounded the corner and, after a moment's surprise, closed in on them. Vion acted swiftly. Flinging himself at the two women, he gave Peri enough start for her to pelt around a corner, putting enough distance between her and the attendants to make any immediate pursuit pointless.

The two women looked at each other. 'Who was that girl, Sib?' they demanded of Vion.

Vion remained silent.

'Perhaps you would like a little sunburn, yes?'

Vion said nothing. The attendant smiled cruelly at him. 'You can go back to the matrons to be put on the sleep list.'

Vion nodded miserably. He looked down the corridor with vague thoughts of escape, but realized both attendants carried ray-sticks.

'You could tell us about the girl who ran away. Maybe that would persuade us to recommend a review,' the other attendant said reasonably.

'Her name's Peri. That's all I know.'

41

'That isn't enough.'

Vion shrugged, then shook his head.

'Return him to the matrons?' the first attendant asked her companion.

'Check with control centre.'

Vion was led away, head down and resigned to his fate.

Rana Zandusia looked around at the gathering that had assembled inside Anzor's TARDIS. Jarmaya and Ulema waited respectfully behind her with two attendants holding ray-sticks in case of disturbance. Sil was greedily taking in every detail of the control systems, while the two Time Lords stood glowering at each other. 'Let us try to travel through the fabric of time, shall we?' she said softly.

'Wait a minute,' the Doctor said. 'Anzor can't drive – he's the worst navigator imaginable. You might wish to go back to primordial slime with him but I don't.'

'I wouldn't tell them anything of importance,' Anzor snorted. 'You're to blame, Doctor Blabbermouth!'

'Me!' the Doctor cried. 'Who was it let them into the TARDIS? That's forbidden, and you know it!'

'I wanted to save damage to my door, that's all!' Anzor retorted. The two Time Lords glared at each other, the Doctor slowly overcoming his long held fear of the school bully.

'This will sound wonderful in your report back to the Council of Gallifrey. Lost – one TARDIS.'

'It isn't lost yet, Doctor.'

The Doctor continued to stare at Anzor, his voice strengthening as he realized that the fear he had felt since his schooldays was no longer necessary.

'Tell these women, Anzor. Tell them about how your TARDIS operates and they will give the details to someone like Sil. He will develop a process of mass production and bring about wilful distortion of the continuum of time.'

Sil laughed delightedly at such a prospect. Anzor scowled at the Doctor ferociously. But before he could reply Rana Zandusia intervened. '*You* also spoke to us, Doctor, before our brain intersector, Ulema, failed through lack of concentrated attention.'

Anzor laughed. 'Blabbed did he? What did he blab about? Let me see!' Anzor reached for a printout sheet held by Ulema, who moved away from his clutching hand.

'Let him see.' Zandusia ordered. The sheet was handed to Anzor, who scanned it rapidly with an expression of scornful glee.

'Hah! You accuse me, Doctor, you talk of me . . . It's here, the formula for time travel!'

'Let me . . .' the Doctor stared at the sheet and turned, with an expression of dismay, to Ulema. 'How did you obtain this?'

Ulema smiled with enjoyment. 'You thought you were so clever! When I was in your mind I could visualize what you were suppressing. I recalled it all later after your little moment of triumph.'

The Doctor bowed in acknowledgement. Sil clapped his hands, making a wet slapping sound. 'Let us test the Doctor's information!'

43

An assistant stepped forward, took the print-out and turned to Rana Zandusia for permission to continue. The tall ruler nodded almost imperceptibly, and the assistant began to make a series of adjustments to the settings. Intent on translating the details of the formula, the young attendant had placed her ray-stick on the console top and Anzor saw the opportunity. With a sudden darting movement he grabbed the stick and fumbled with its control trigger, sending a searing ray of energy that narrowly missed the Doctor. Scattering in panic the party of women retreated through the door of the TARDIS. Only the Doctor stood his ground. 'Anzor, please listen to me.'

'Shut up, Doctor, you are cluttering up my TARDIS!'

'Anzor, *listen!*'

'No. It is your turn to do that. Sorry I can't administer the beating you deserve, but when I get back to Gallifrey, I will blacken your name for all time.' Anzor began to laugh with malice and enjoyment.

The Doctor tried to interrupt once more.

'Please . . .'

'Out!' Anzor gestured with the energy weapon.

The Doctor eyed the ray-stick nervously. Raising his hands in a gesture of surrender, he backed out of the TARDIS. The gnarled door panel closed on Anzor's gloating face, grinning at him with malicious triumph.

Shaking his head the Doctor turned away as the party of angry women led by Zandusia and Sil surrounded him. Before anyone could speak the trumpeting sound of dematerialization filled the room. Terrified, the women backed away.

'What?' Zandusia cried in fear.

'TARDIS dematerialization,' the Doctor said.

'Then your friend has escaped.'

The Doctor looked around at the distraught faces about him.

'Not really. I played a trick – a double bluff. Ulema, I knew you had registered that formula, taken it from my mind. Those instructions were designed to take Anzor's TARDIS on a very slow ride back to the beginning of time. I thought that was the best solution, to take Anzor's TARDIS out of your reach for ever.'

Ulema was stunned. 'But Anzor can halt your setting. He can change course, surely?'

The Doctor looked thoughtfully at the space where the ancient oak had stood.

'I doubt it. He's not a skilled navigator. Ah, well, he can try bullying molluscs and pterodactyls, or make a study of mesozoic slime mould,' the Doctor said cheerfully.

Zandusia regarded the Time Lord with a mixture of anger and respect.

'We must watch you closely, Doctor. That was a complex trap we almost stepped into.'

Sil stared at the Doctor with loathing. 'He is tricky as a troupe of monkeys. He should be killed for the treachery and corruption he has brought to your pure world of beauty and grace!'

'He will be consigned to sleep after we locate and

reveal the secrets of his TARDIS,' Zandusia replied. Sil realised the truth of this, his anger fading.

'Of course, Rana, I had forgotten. There must be another TARDIS, and we know how to enter it, thanks to Anzor!'

The Doctor smiled blandly. 'I can't remember where I left my TARDIS. Sorry. Anyway its security lock is different to dear old Anzor's.'

'Check where the Matrons found him, and search back from there. It shouldn't be far away.' The Rana's orders were crisp and decisive.

The Doctor smiled engagingly and tried to divert the direction of the search. 'Unless we travelled many miles before meeting those child minders of yours.'

The Rana was not to be so easily fooled. 'We will search back to the regions of ice, if necessary, Doctor.'

'Ice regions? I thought Magnus was warm and wet all over.'

'No, ice exists in the polar regions.'

'Oh.' The Doctor's brow furrowed.

'It would save us all a great deal of bother and you, particularly, a great deal of discomfort if you would tell us how your time machine operates.'

Maintaining the polite tone of the exchange the Doctor said: 'I will not tell you the secrets of time travel.'

Jarmaya, more impetuous than her leader, burst out vehemently: 'You will! The peace of our planet depends on our discovering your secrets!'

The Rana restrained Jarmaya with a light touch. 'You see, Doctor, we are already at war. The Salvakian males are preparing to invade. They have been focusing strange forces upon our planet causing climatic disturbance.'

'In what way?' the Doctor asked sharply.

'The levels of our oceans rise, our pattern of weather changes. What was a calm temperate climate is undergoing unpredictable changes.'

'Why is this happening? *How* is this happening?'

Rana shrugged. 'We don't know. It seems a surprising development for the men of Salvak. But who else could it be?'

'Mmm. Presumably the ice caps are melting – hence the change in climate.'

Jarmaya nodded in agreement. 'We have located definite heat focus from space.'

'I did notice a space ship oribiting.'

Zandusia interrupted, her large eyes clouding with something akin to hatred. 'That would be the Salvakians. You see, they must be stopped – you *must* help us. We have a paradise, a new Earth here, peace, order, beauty. I will not let it go down before savage masculine barbarity.'

In answer to the woman's steely determination the Doctor mildly replied: 'Is that necessarily one and the same thing?'

Fire flared in the green eyes of the Rana. 'Yes – show me a world dominated by males and I will show you blood and fire and war!'

The women present, stirred by their leader's tone, gave their support in a chorus of affirmation. Zandusia continued: 'By a fortunate chance, God in Her wisdom has ensured that no male of our species can exist on the surface of Magnus. I fear the Salvakians may have discovered how they can survive here. They must be halted by whatever means necessary!'

'Except for time subversion, you mean,' the Doctor dryly commented.

'That would save us from turning our powers of invention to creating the engines of war.'

'Which would bring fire and blood and war.'

'It would not be our fault but yours, Doctor. Believe me, we will fight to the death.'

The Doctor did not reply. Jarmaya, presuming his silence to mean that he was considering the matter, made an appeal for help. 'Help us, Doctor. Save us from the necessity of such a war.'

'I cannot,' the Doctor said. 'It is forbidden.'

'Then we must try other methods to gain that information from you,' the Rana said, her voice cold with determination.

6

Peri had wandered through the bewilderingly similar corridors and apartments of the Rana's palace, becoming increasingly uncertain of her direction and purpose. At one point she had entered a throne room containing an ancient oak tree. Puzzled, she had circled this, but deduced nothing from its appearance, little guessing that the Doctor and the Magnusian women had been inside, together with Sil and Anzor. Disconsolately, Peri had wandered back into the palace. Peeping into various rooms she saw only sleeping servants. Finding no sign of the Doctor or Vion, Peri decided to leave the palace and return the way she had travelled in the hope of finding or perhaps even saving Vion.

In the Zandusia's throne room the Rana regarded the surprisingly cheerful Doctor. Sil, annoyed by the Time Lord's calm, began to splutter with rage. 'Why are we waiting? Waste not an hour. Try torture, anything!'

'We do not stoop to such methods, Sil. We will all concentrate our mental power upon him. Then he will succumb.'

'What . . .?' Sil watched amazed as all but one of the women closed their eyes and went into a trance-like state. One attendant stayed watching the Doctor, her force stick ready to prevent any dash for freedom. The Doctor grinned at Sil. Then the grin fell away as a wave of power assailed his mind.

The mental voices of the psychic women urged him to reveal his secrets of time travel. The furies were at first threatening, then flattering. Their intellects picked through his mind, searching for the key to overcome his resistance.

It would be so easy to say yes they told him in voices dripping with honeyed persuasion, *yes, why not break the one rule of Gallifrey you have always obeyed.*

Always obeyed, always obeyed, the Doctor's thoughts came back to them, hanging on to the words as a man clinging on to the only ledge on a wind-torn cliff face. *What*, he thought, *if they ever turn this power to hate or coercion?*

What if, indeed? the voices asked, then showed him. In the Doctor's mind each woman's intellect became a stab of terror, expanding, merging into a single beam of primal fear. There was only one escape. The Doctor fell to the floor, unconscious, having found the only way to save his sanity. The circle of women opened their eyes, their mood angry. Their prey had escaped!

'Bring him round. Bring him round,' Sil shrilled. 'Splash water! Splash water!'

'Pointless,' Rana Zandusia replied. 'If he can escape into unconsciousness once he can do it again.'

Then Sil remembered something. 'The girl! That horrible looking girl. He used to travel with a cheeky young miss! *That* is why he was so calm – he expects rescue!'

An attendant stepped forward, bowed to the Rana. 'There was a report of a girl wandering the palace without permission.'

'Was she captured?' Zandusia asked.

'No. She ran away.'

'We sometimes get girls from the maternity units straying into the palace grounds,' Jarmaya said.

'Investigate this,' Zandusia ordered. 'Begin the search for the TARDIS. Use all patrol personnel. Check any reports of sightings.'

'Yes, Rana.' Jarmaya hurried away.

Sil looked approvingly across the body of the Doctor. 'At last you act like a leader. You have the ability – now you must increase your will, Rana.'

The words caught the Rana's interest.

'Have you known many leaders, Sil?'

'Oh, many, many, believe me. But you, Rana, you could be the greatest of them all.'

'Subtle, isn't he?' said a voice from the floor. Zandusia and Sil watched as the Doctor sat up then jumped to his feet. 'Don't listen to him, Rana,' the Doctor said as he yawned and stretched.

Sil's voice grated with rage. 'Why not? Why not!'

'Why are you here, Sil?' the Doctor asked.

'My business.'

'What is there on Magnus for money mad creatures like him?' the Doctor asked.

Before the Rana could reply Sil's bitterness burst forth. 'Because I am now a subordinate thanks to you and your interference in my moneymaking plans for Varos.'

'Oh, yes . . .' the Doctor said with irony. 'Varos. What a fun place that was.'

'Sil,' the Rana interrupted softly. 'Tell me of the leaders you have known.'

Sil thought back through his career as a plenipotentiary of Thoros Beta. 'Kings, queens, emperors, governors, blood royals and some who became royal by taking power.'

'All Sil's associates tend to share one thing in common,' the Doctor quietly interjected.

'And what is that, Doctor?' Sil asked.

'Ending up dead, Sil,' the Doctor replied.

The beautiful ruler of Magnus Epsilon adjusted her robes. It was difficult to decide whose words had made the greater impact. 'Let us find your TARDIS, Doctor.' She turned away, her entourage fluttering about her as they left the throne room.

Peri had failed to find Vion but had shadowed a matron hurrying to her night work in the underground dormitory area where the boys were held captive. From her vantage point by the dormitory entrance Peri could see, behind a locked metal grille, rows of narrow beds and on one of them, Vion sitting up and staring blankly ahead. This side of the grille another matron sat nodding sleepily, a bunch of keys laid on a

table before her. Peri decided that if the drowsy
matron did fall asleep she would attempt a rescue.
The matron's head drooped, fell, raised itself, then
went through the whole sequence again. Just as Peri
was about to give the whole attempt up as hopeless
she realized that the matron was asleep.

Carefully Peri edged towards the table and the
bunch of keys that could release Vion from captivity.
Step by careful step she advanced towards the table.
Two paces away the woman stirred. Caught in the
open, Peri could hear her heart thumping up into her
throat. She halted, waiting for the eyes to open, the
shout to come, the force stick of the matron to be
raised in anger. But then the head drooped and Peri
could breathe again.

On the other side of the grille Vion had started with
excitement. He had noticed Peri's progress and now
began to move quietly towards her through the lines
of sleeping boys. Peri closed her hand over the keys
and lifted them as slowly as she dared. A chinking
sound caused her a moment's heart-stopping alarm,
but the matron slept on.

Tiptoeing to the grille Peri tried several keys without success before the lock finally turned. Vion opened
the grille, sliding its cold metal mesh back with great
care. When there was room he slipped through and to
Peri's consternation headed purposefully for the sleeping matron. Circling behind her Vion reached down
to her belt. With great delicacy and the skill of a
natural pickpocket he slowly extracted the force stick
from the carrying pouch attached to the matron's belt.
Meanwhile Peri closed the grille, relocked it and

returned the keys to the table in more or less the same position as before.

Peri and Vion looked momentarily at each other across the head of the sleeping matron. A sudden snore startled them into movement. With Vion holding the force stick at the ready they hurried out of sight. After a moment the matron woke up, saw nothing amiss and lapsed back into dreamland.

In the darkness of the underworld passageways Vion and Peri halted to catch their breath. Vion spoke with some amazement. 'Why risk your freedom? I am on their sleep list. I was to be eliminated, never to wake up again.'

'Why is that? What have you done that any normal boy wouldn't do?'

Vion shook his head. 'You don't understand how it is. I don't know where you come come from. Where do you come from?' He spoke wonderingly, his dark eyes questioning.

Peri thought of Earth and of the best way to convey the strange experience of time travel. It seemed a daunting task so she opted for simplicity. 'Another world, another time; a planet where women are mostly treated less well than men.'

Vion shook his head in disbelief but said nothing.

Vion and Peri began to walk at a more leisurely pace, the teenage boy holding the force stick before him as a protection against any possible dangers. He began to brood as they walked along the dark passage. 'Anyone who shows signs of what the matrons call overt manhood is weeded out. Only the docile are allowed to survive for use in the repro-labs.'

Suddenly the enormity of the forces ranged against him made Vion quail. 'Give yourself up, Peri!' he burst out. 'Say I forced you to help, they'll find a place in their world of women for you. You're of their kind, they'll forgive you.'

'Hey, stop it!' Peri put an arm around the boy's shoulders. 'Let's find the Doctor. I couldn't see him anywhere in that palace.'

'Where would he be, the Doctor?'

'That's a good question, Vion.' Peri considered, then came up with the only thing she could think of. 'Let's try to get back to the TARDIS. Maybe he'll turn up there.'

'His manifestation, yes?' Vion pondered. 'It's not that far and at least I have this to protect you with.' He brandished the force stick and with some vigour in his step set off down the passageway with Peri following more in hope than with any real expectation of finding the Doctor.

55

7

The police box was surrounded by a group of attendants, guards and members of the court of Rana Zandusia. The Rana and the Doctor stood together; like everyone present they were watching a girl locksmith testing a number of different keys on the TARDIS door. When the lock refused to give way to the various combinations, the Doctor commented to Zandusia, 'One TARDIS is not the same as another.'

The Rana seemed undismayed. 'We have applied a calculated variant to each formula, used the Devlin principle of randomized mathematical probability and have the most likely key combinations to try . . . ah!' The Rana had noticed the last key the attendant had tried almost turned the lock.

'That means nothing,' the Doctor said, perhaps a trifle over hastily.

The Rana smiled mockingly. 'No? We will now work on that last shape and code signal so that the next batch will produce the key to all your secrets of time travel, Doctor.'

'Or not,' the Doctor said with more confidence than he was feeling.

'Tell us now, Doctor. Discovery is inevitable.'

'Tell them nothing, Doctor!' Peri's voice rang out. The group at the TARDIS swung round to face the force stick held unwaveringly by Vion.

'Peri!' the Doctor called. 'About time. I wondered where you had got to. Hardly dared ask, as you can imagine.'

'I can,' Peri said, looking at the circle of colourfully dressed exotic women gathered around the Doctor. 'Quite a hen party, hey Doc?'

The Rana began to assert her authority now that the first shock of surprise had abated. 'Throw down that stick, boy, this very moment. I, Rana Zandusia command it!'

Peri saw the force stick waver under the Rana's command. The circle of women began to focus their mental concentration. The Doctor, having felt the power that could be exerted, moved quickly to avert disaster.

'Let's get out of here. Peri, Vion, move!' Reacting to the urgency in the Doctor's voice Peri pushed Vion away in the direction of the nearest bolt hole.

The Doctor, pausing only to lift the TARDIS keys from the grasp of the young locksmith, ran after Peri and Vion and disappeared from the view of the women who hesitated, waiting for orders.

'Bring them to me!' Zandusia yelled with rage, her voice cracking like a whip. Hastily the attendants began to give chase, running into the passageway that the Doctor and his companions had just taken. The light was poor and there was no sign of the Doctor. Soon the half dozen attendants came to a division of passageways that veered away into the darkness. After a slight pause of indecision the pursuers split into two groups and carried on their hunt for the three fugitives who had dared to thwart the will of the Rana Zandusia.

As soon as the corridors were quiet the Doctor dropped down from a ledge above the fork in the passageways. Peri followed and helped Vion down in her turn.

'Useful ledge that, Vion,' she said.

'Yes, we know the nooks and crannies around here. It's our world, underground.'

'Let's get back to the TARDIS and get out of here,' Peri urged the Doctor.

The Doctor shook his head. 'There'll be some women left to guard it. No, there are things happening on Magnus that I neither understand nor like. I need answers to lots of questions.'

'You mean revelations.'

'Revelations?' the Doctor glanced down at Vion.

'Yes. You are the chosen ones, aren't you?'

'Vion, I don't know what you mean.'

Vion gazed at the Doctor, his eyes alive with excitement.

'There is a hope, a legend that once men could live and work above, that they and women could exist together and that one day this togetherness would happen again.'

'Perhaps it will, in time.'

Vion shook his head. 'You saw the Rana: she hates us all.'

'That Amazon Queen?' Peri asked the Doctor.

'Yes. She is beginning to enjoy her power a little too much. We must teach her that co-operation between the sexes is worth encouraging.'

'I think moving from here is more pressing, Doctor. Those women with the nasty force sticks should be on their way back any time now.' Peri shivered.

'Yes. Where are we? East? West?' the Doctor turned to Vion.

'North.'

'Ah. That's why it seems cooler.'

'Yes.' Vion indicated another smaller tunnel and ducked down inside. The rocky floor sloped downwards then opened out a little to allow them to walk without stooping. The air seemed to have a chill of frost on it. Vion shivered. 'South of here, where the main cities are, it is warm all of the time. I saw a book belonging to the matrons once; it had pictures of white buildings, bright orange flowers hanging from trees, blue skies and over it all a bright sun burning down.' A slight tremor came into the boy's voice as he pronounced the fearful word 'sun'.

'But the male children are kept here in the north. Why?'

'Because it's safer for us to be kept up here. A little longer night, a little less day.'

'I see,' the Doctor said, then walked for a while without speaking, lost in speculative thought.

59

'Brr . . .' Peri said, feeling suddenly chilled through her thin T-shirt. 'I'm freezing.'

'How far are we from the ice-cap region, Vion?' asked the Doctor.

Vion considered. 'Not far. I have been this way before, to where the tunnels turn to solid ice.'

'Good,' the Doctor said briskly. 'Take us there, please.'

'What!' Peri could not believe what she was hearing.

'No one lives there,' Vion said, equally puzzled.

The Doctor made no reply but continued to walk along at a fast pace between walls now lined with hoar frost.

Peri tried again. 'Cold and ice. Who could live there, Doctor?'

'Yes. Quite. Who would want to?'

'Unless they're crazy.' Peri almost added *Like you*. But there was something in the Doctor's expression that made her change her mind.

'Doctor . . .' Vion started, but the Doctor increased his pace. Vion decided to save his breath as he hurried to keep up with the purposeful Doctor.

'Fools, idiots!'

Jarmaya tried to soothe the angry green slug that was gesticulating and bouncing up and down in his water tank. 'We only need to recreate the keys. Try them again. This Doctor can run around till he finds there's nothing but frostbite to look forward to. Remember, Sil, we have his TARDIS.'

'Yes.' Sil simmered down a little while Rana Zandusia issued orders for the TARDIS to be guarded by four armed attendants.

'Guard it with your lives!' Sil could not resist adding.

'They will.' Zandusia stared at the irate Sil. 'We must talk.'

'Yes, your Majesty.'

'Rana.'

'As yet, Majesty, as yet.' There was a pause. Zandusia regarded the Thoros Betan.

'Sil, I am curious about your purchase of land and properties. I have meant to ask you. Well?'

'Er, property?' Sil looked uneasily up at the Rana. He had not expected this.

'Most things come to my attention, Sil.'

'Well . . .' Sil tried to think of a reason to hide the true purpose of his purchases. 'I am in the business of making business wherever I find myself,' he said rather weakly.

'Factory space. Commissioning machinery for manufacturing heavy woollen garments, blankets, *heating* appliances, here on Magnus?'

'You are well informed,' Sil spluttered.

Zandusia smiled. 'Yes, but then your foolishness is the talk of Magnus.'

'I plan to export, to, er, Salvak, yes, that's it.'

'Salvak!' the Rana scowled at the hated name. Her expression became fierce with hatred and suspicion.

'After, after they are defeated, of course.' Sil babbled hastily. 'They are not so fortunate as to climate are they not?'

'No. Their planet is not as warm as ours,' the Rana laughed. 'It is warmer. Arid. You have been duped, Sil; who told you the Salvakians would require heating appliances?'

'That Time Lord, Anzor.' Sil looked downcast.

'You have been fooled, Sil.'

'Yes, Rana,' said Sil, trying to look even more upset.

'Serve you right for not referring your questions to me.'

'Yes, your Majesty, I will in future. Thank you so very much.'

Zandusia, now in better humour, smiled and relaxed, signalling permission for the courtiers to laugh derisively over Sil's foolishness. Giggling, Zandusia and her followers moved away towards the passage that would return them to the surface.

Sil waited for his woman bearers to lift him so that he, too, could follow. No one heard him mutter secretly to himself as the women's laughter drifted back to him. 'In future, did you say, my Lady Zandusia? In future, Madam, you will crawl to me!'

Then he laughed, and the gurgling sound of mad humour reverberated throughout the cavern as he was borne away.

8

The Doctor, Peri and Vion had travelled northwards, finding the temperature becoming ever colder as they advanced. Now the walls had turned into the pale blue of solid ice. Silently they paused to examine the smooth walls and to survey the widening ice tunnel that loomed ahead of them. Vion was the first to speak.

'This is a new excavation. I'm sure the tunnel ended about here. This ice section is new.'

'Why is it so large?' asked Peri, rubbing arms covered in goose bumps.

'Yes.' Vion added. 'It's much larger than the rock passage behind.'

'Let's find out,' the Doctor said and strode down into the corridor of solid ice.

Hurrying along at speed, trying to keep warm, Peri became aware of a shifting in the structure of the ice around them. 'Doctor, is this safe?'

'Bit of pressure, that's all.'

'I'm freezing.'

'That'll be the ice, I expect.'

Before Peri could give a retort there was a loud crack from directly above them. 'Let's go back!' Peri urged.

'No, Peri. We must find out what this leads to.'

They followed the curve of the corridor into a hollow chamber carved from the ice. At the centre of this stood a large T-shaped device that, although crudely made, had a profusion of multi-coloured wires running away from input points. These disappeared into a large tunnel that had been bored to make an entrance into the ice wall on the opposite side of the chamber. The Doctor, curious as always, was the first to approach the waist-high device with its glowing innards of complex technology. He had time for only a brief examination of the device before a gasp from Peri brought his attention to a split in the roof of the cavern. Almost immediately there was a rumbling sound and a cascade of ice tumbled down into the chamber blocking the way ahead. The Doctor returned, unperturbed, to his examination of the strange device.

'Doctor!' Peri was scared of another ice fall.

'Quiet. I'm trying to concentrate.'

'Doctor!' Peri stared at the ceiling of ice bulging above them.

'Peri, recognise what this device is?'

'No.' Was that crack widening right above them?

'This is like a nuclear detonator. Primitive but effective.'

'You mean we are standing next to an atom bomb!'

'No. Just the detonator.'

As the Doctor pored over the system of wiring around the central column he nodded with satisfaction. 'Yes, an isotope of lithium set in what must be deuterium tritium.' He straightened, an expression of consternation appearing on his face.

'I can hardly . . . Oh, no . . .!'

'What, Doctor?'

This detonator is large enough for a hydrogen bomb of massive proportions – a bomb big enough perhaps to destroy all of Magnus!'

'And us?'

'Of course!'

'Who would want to do that?' Vion asked bewilderedly.

Almost as if in reply there was the sound of crashing from the direction of the ice fall that had blocked the far corridor. Then the fallen ice burst apart, and a green shape began to emerge as the ice splayed and was then thrust aside with frightening force. Finally the figure broke through and came lumbering towards them, clumps of ice falling from his barrel chest.

'No!' Peri screamed, seeing the helmeted head.

'Wh . . . what is that?' Vion stuttered as the giant biped lurched down upon them.

'Ice Warriors!' the Doctor cried in realization and held his head. 'That space ship out there is the flagship of the Grand Marshal!'

'Doctor!' Peri yelled, but it was too late. Vion managed to fire a ray from the force stick he carried but the bolt glanced harmlessly from the Ice Warrior's armoured chest. With a backhand blow of its clamped fist the Doctor was swept aside. Vion began to run away but before Peri could do likewise she found herself engulfed and lifted by the massive arm of the Ice Warrior. Screaming and kicking helplessly Peri saw the monster bend down and with his free hand strike down at the detonator. With the thud of contact the device began to emit an eerie crimson glow. The spill of intermittent light shone fitfully on the Doctor's face as he lay unconscious beside the pulsing detonator.

The Ice Warrior turned and, carrying Peri in his arms, began to lumber away back into the cold heart of the polar ice cap.

9

'Doctor! Doctor!' Vion had crawled to the uncon-scious Time Lord and was desperately trying to revive him. Finding no response Vion lifted two large lumps of ice and held a piece on either side of the Doctor's temples. Almost immediately there was a response.

'Uh. Wha . . .?'

The Doctor smiled up at the young man who peered down at him anxiously.

'Must keep a cool head from now on, Vion. I, er, think I'm cool enough now.'

'Sorry.' Vion drew the ice lumps away hurriedly.

'Thanks.' The Doctor sat up and looked groggily about him. 'Where's Peri?'

'That green ice thing took her away with him,' Vion said worriedly, wondering why the Doctor seemed to be ignoring the detonator that was ticking, buzzing and glowing with increasing intensity.

'Is the monster from Salvak, Doctor?'

'No, planet Mars to be precise. A long, long time

ago. I thought they were extinct.' Still dazed by the blow from the massive Ice Warrior, the Doctor continued vaguely, 'What can throwbacks to the ice age want on a warm world like Magnus?'

Vion did not know. He watched the Doctor haul himself to his feet using the active detonator as a means of leverage. The Time Lord swayed slightly, shook his head once more then added, as an afterthought, 'Nothing on Magnus for such creatures except slow sleepy death.' He glanced vaguely about him. 'Peri, which way did she go?'

Vion was searching among the fragments of shattered ice. He looked up and pointed towards the opening opposite.

'Ah. Thank you.' The Doctor began to wander away.

Vion found the force stick for which he had been searching and called urgently across the ice cavern. 'Doctor, shouldn't we do something about this?'

The Time Lord turned and stared back at the young man illuminated by the flashing crimson light from the detonator. 'Oh, yes, I knew there was something else.' He crossed to the detonator and examined the flow of power as it zig-zagged through the conduits that led to the main isotopic chamber. To Vion the Doctor seemed to enter a trance of concentration that lasted a long time. Then, with a sigh, the Doctor straightened. 'What a surprise. Quite advanced technology of its type. Something that can't be allowed to function, of course.' The Doctor pressed a reset switch and instantly the detonator eased down to a more quiescent state. The Time Lord strolled away towards the exit from the chamber.

Vion hurried to join him. Glancing up at the Doctor, Vion said tentatively, 'Are you all right?'

'Oh, yes.'

Vion didn't press the matter further. With this strangely eccentric visitor you had no way of knowing whether his odd behaviour was usual or caused by the fearsome blow struck by the green-skinned monster who had descended upon them. Vion kept silent and warily followed the Doctor as they journeyed further and further into the passage that must have been bored into the heart of the polar region by the Ice Warriors.

Vedikael, commander of the Ice Warriors, stood to attention before a communications unit screen. His right fist was clenched across to his left shoulder in respectful salute to the speckled head that filled the screen before him. The reedy voice of the Grand Marshal floated into the chamber that had been gouged from the deep ice of the polar ice face. Other Ice Warriors who had been lumbering around checking the various monitoring units contained in the chamber, stiffened to attention at the sound of their ruler's voice.

'Vedikael, are all systems functioning for the required nuclear experiment?'

'Yes, Grand Marshal.' The voice was rasping and had a wheeze to it. The eyes of Vedikael glowed fanatically, a red blur behind the protective eye shades set into his helmet. 'All detonating units are now in a state of armed readiness, Grand Marshal.'

'Good.' On the screen the wizened head nodded. 'The orbital position of Magnus Epsilon will be favourable in one hour's time. Prepare for maximum power then.'

'It will be done, Grand Marshall!'

'Do not fail. The survival of our entire race depends on the success of your mission.'

'We will not fail!'

The screen cleared as the link to the Martian space ship was ended. Vedikael turned to face Skaag, who had been waiting patiently for the attention of his commander.

'We have failure in number three detonator,' Skaag hissed.

'Ice fall?'

'Perhaps.'

'Check.' Vedikael paused at the sight of Jarga carrying what seemed like an Earthling woman in his arms.

'Let me go you, you . . .!' the creature was screaming in its shrill voice.

Vedikael completed her sentence with a tinge of pleasure in his throaty voice. 'Giant. Monster. Reptile?'

'Yes!' Peri said defiantly as Jarga lowered her to the floor.

'Who is this?' the commander asked.

'Found at the edge of the ice-cap tunnels.'

Peri felt the red eyes surveying her. She had to listen hard to the hissing voice that came from the

70

leader of the monsters. When she did comprehend the words she became even more chilled than before.

'Why bring a human here? Destroy her at once!'

'Commander,' Jarga said obediently and made an adjustment to the weapon that seemed to be built into his right forearm. The device was levelled at Peri who realized she had only a fleeting moment to save her life.

'No. Wait!' she pleaded.

'Why wait? You are of no use to us.' Vedikael spoke with complete disinterest.

'I can help you!' Peri blurted out, desperately sensing that the aliens were utterly self-seeking.

She was right. Vedikael regarded her with a hint of interest. 'How can you help us?'

'Because I know the routes of the underground passageways!'

The commander smiled. 'Soon there will be no need for us to use them. No need for us to hide underground.'

'I can help you with the women who rule Magnus!'

'Those who survive will accept our orders or perish like you.' Vedikael motioned to Jarga.

Peri stared at the clumsy hands of her executioner and plunged into what could be the last gamble of her life. 'These . . . these . . .' she waggled her long dexterous fingers. 'Women's fingers, able to manipulate Magnusian technology.'

'We can . . .' Jarga began.

'No, not with those great clumsy things. What are they, clamps not fingers?'

Vedikael signed to Jarga to delay the despatch of the shapely girl.

'You are a trained technological operator?' he asked.

'Sure,' Peri lied. 'Fully trained, the best. First class degree in TARDIS technology, UCLA.'

Vedikael hissed ominously. Peri wondered if she had blundered through too much elaboration. 'If you are lying . . .' the commander warned.

'Yeah, sure, I'll be obliterated.' Peri shivered as the weapon arm of the Ice Warrior called Jarga was lowered.

'Go, examine detonator three,' the commander ordered. With a salute Jarga and Skaag lumbered away.

Peri spotted a pile of what looked like hides heaped in a corner. 'Hey!'

Vedikael, about to consult a VDU screen turned in annoyance. 'You address me as Commander Vedikael if you ever dare speak to me at all.'

'Yes . . .' Peri's teeth began to chatter. Her feet felt numb and dead with cold. She pointed at the skins. 'Can I . . . I'm so cold.'

'Oh, yes, you creatures cannot enjoy the cold, can you?' Vedikael mocked the shivering girl.

'Y-you c-could say!'

'The ice is our friend.'

'Please!'

'Take them. Those who wore those clothes have no further need for warmth!' Vedikael laughed harshly causing the other Ice Warriors to hiss gleefully in unison from their work stations.

Peri lifted the first tunic. It was fur-lined, but with a burnt patch in the centre of the back. It was large when she slipped it on but with rolled-up sleeves it would do. After searching further through the pile she managed to find a small pair of leggings that fitted her. Wearing the protective clothing Peri felt better and turned her thoughts to the problem of escaping from the alien monsters who seemed ruthlessly intent on bringing nuclear destruction to Magnus Epsilon.

Trudging along, Vion wondered if the Doctor would ever speak again. He sensed that his companion was trying to come to terms with the extraordinary events and decided that it was better to remain silent for the moment. The Time Lord was deep in thought, no doubt turning over the problem of what the Ice Warriors were doing here.

'Perhaps . . .' said the Doctor when a gasp from Vion warned him that two giant Ice Warriors were crunching towards them.

'Run!' the Doctor shouted as the leading Ice Warrior levelled its weapon arm. Skittering on the slippery ice floor, Vion and the Doctor headed precariously for a bend in the blue walls of the passage. The tip of Skaag's sonic weapon glowed and fired; a wave of invisible energy shot down the passageway, smashing into the wall of ice beyond the curve that had saved Vion and the Doctor from certain death. Groaning in protest at the assault, a crack appeared in the domed ceiling of the tunnel and slivers of ice began to fall as the two Ice Warriors lumbered in pursuit of the Doctor and Vion.

10

Further south, in an underground chamber, the defences of the Doctor's TARDIS were about to be breached.

'This one,' Rana Zandusia breathed as Jarmaya tried a further combination key.

'Yes!' Zandusia cried exultantly as the TARDIS door opened silently. Applause, led by Sil, echoed around the chamber as Zandusia entered the old blue police box.

'Hurry, me next!' Sil urged his carriers. Dutifully, the two attendants carried the excited Sil towards the TARDIS.

Inside, Zandusia and Jarmaya looked round the interior of the control room, staring at the inert driving column and the blank viewing screen.

'Tell the sisters of science their work may now begin,' Zandusia ordered.

'Yes, Rana,' Jarmaya replied. 'They know how

important discovering the secrets of time travel is to our future.'

'Yes. Yes.' Sil added gleefully as he joined them. 'Then we will be able to market the Doctor's secrets for fatsi-fatsi profit! With such ultimate wealth you will be Queen of Universal Plenty!'

Zandusia remained calm at the prospect. 'First we must divert the research of our enemies on Salvak: prevent them discovering the antidote that will allow them to invade us. Only then, Sil, may you have the franchise to sell the goods you wish.'

'Of course, Rana, of course.'

Sil watched the Rana and her half dozen courtiers wander away chattering, commenting on the strange inner world of the TARDIS. Finding himself alone apart from his bearers Sil could not contain his joy at the prospects the secrets of time travel would create for someone as greedy as himself.

'First, first, what will I do first?' he asked himself with a gloating cackle.

'Yes, oh, yes, I will transport myself ahead in time to the headquarters of Galactic Lotteries, find out the ten year billion credit-winning ticket number then send myself back in time to buy, beg, steal that number. Then, then I will build a fleet of time-ships and plunder the riches of all time!'

Driven into a surge of wild joy Sil pressed various switches before him. At once the cylindrical driving column responded, rising and falling in flight. Frightened, Sil gulped in terror and stabbed his stubby fingers at the switches again. The driving column became inert once more.

'What's happening?' the voice of Jarmaya demanded. 'Who was playing with the time controls?'

One of Sil's attendants pointed an accusing finger at the squirming Thoros Betan.

'Nothing happened. I was simply testing to see if the time machine was functioning. Nothing happened, I'm sure.'

'Is everyone unharmed?' The Rana had joined Jarmaya.

'Yes, yes,' Sil assured her. 'Set fair for handsome profit, Rana.'

Despite his bluster the women sensed an unease in Sil. Jarmaya spoke decisively. 'Let us check outside.'

'All I did was . . .' Sil demonstrated by again touching the controls before him. This time the viewing screen activated.

'Stop!' Jarmaya yelled at Sil.

'Look!' Zandusia pointed at the viewing screen which showed a desolate landscape of ash-covered gutted buildings and the rubble of devastation.

'Where is that?' Sil asked the group about him.

After a silence Zandusia spoke in a dull tone. 'I know the shape of that landscape. That range of mountains, they are the heights of Bassan.'

A shock of recognition ran through the assembled women.

'Then, those fallen buildings . . .' Jarmaya started.

'. . . are all that remains of my winter palace.'

Sil started to wriggle with agitation. 'All I did was . . . Ah, this TARDIS is so very hostile to my person!'

'Shut up!' Jarmaya snapped at Sil before addressing her leader. 'I believe Sil must have moved us forward in time. What we are seeing out there is how Magnus will appear in the future.'

The realization brought a horrified reaction from the Rana. 'Devastated, blasted, destroyed?'

'It cannot be too far in the future,' Sil said. 'That column thing hardly lifted at all.'

Rana Zandusia paced back to the wall and turned. 'So all will be lost. Everything we have must perish. The men from Salvak must win. We women must submit or die?'

'No, Rana.' Jarmaya hurried to offer comfort to her ruler. 'I have worked with our sisters who are exploring and researching time travel; what we see out there is what will happen if factors operating now remain unaltered.' Jarmaya paused. All present hung on her words, seeking hope that somehow the destruction shown on the screen might be averted. 'There must be multi-layers and infinite combinations of future time possibility,' Jarmaya concluded.

Rana Zandusia considered. 'But for now we are marooned here. Hours, days, maybe weeks ahead of where we were only minutes ago?'

'Yes, Rana. My guess is perhaps only hours ahead.'

The Rana stared at the screen and its unchanging desolate scene. 'What can have happened and so quickly?' she asked Jarmaya, who shook her head in reply then said slowly, 'The answer to that must lie during the past few hours. The catastrophe must have happened then.'

In the ice tunnels the Doctor and Vion had outdistanced the cumbersome Ice Warriors and reached the site of the disarmed detonator. A little beyond the device, they huddled behind a mound of fallen ice and after a short time peeped over to see Jarga and Skaag bent over the device, trying to discover why it was no longer working.

The Doctor signed for Vion to circle and return back the way they had come. They had almost reached the opening before Skaag glanced up and saw them.

'There!' he rasped and began to slog across the chamber in pursuit, leaving Jarga with the task of reactivating nuclear detonator number three.

Further north, behind the main control chamber, was a series of ice grottoes used by the Ice Warriors to store supplies and prisoners. Accompanied by Craag, a massive Ice Warrior some eight feet in height, Peri soon found herself thrust into a small igloo-like space. Another warrior, Farn, lumbered into view, sonic weapon armed and ready to fire. The arm relaxed as he saluted the approach of Craag.

'Guard the prisoners closely. Detonation is now imminent,' Craag ordered hoarsely.

'Yes, of course!'

Inside the hut Peri became aware that she was not alone. A low voice sounded. A male voice. A human voice! 'Sira! Is it . . . can it be?' the voice said.

'Sira . . .?' Peri asked tremulously.

'Yes, who are you?' The voice became fierce and threatening. Peri became aware that there were four others beside herself in the ice hut. Her eyes strained to bring detail to the shapes that now loomed towards her.

'Who are you?' another voice asked. 'And why are you wearing the clothes that belonged to Sira?'

'I was given them by those, those . . .'

'Ice Warriors. You are a prisoner too?'

'Yes.' Peri saw a handsome, bearded man, swathed in animal hides like herself.

'My name is Ishka; I am sorry if I frightened you. You have been given the clothing of the woman who accompanied us on our expedition from Salvak.'

'Ah.' Peri understood a little more of the situation.

'Let me see.' Another bearded man thrust his face into hers and regarded her closely. 'At last we meet a woman of Magnus. A warrior woman.'

'Who, me?' Peri asked, incredulously.

'On Salvak you women are legend.'

'You are Salvakians?'

'Yes. I am Ishka, this Hussa, there Rodan and . . .'

'Dabasir,' a quieter voice said.

Peri acknowledged the four men. 'My name is Peri.'

'You must think us savages,' Dabasir said. 'These animal skins, beards, they have become necessary for our survival.'

'You are part of the invading force?'

Hussa smiled grimly. 'What remains of it. Our spacecraft was destroyed by those aliens. A group of us managed to escape in a recon module, but we were captured again and brought here to assist in the Ice Warriors's plan to destroy Magnus.'

'How?' Peri asked, puzzled.

'Have you not seen their detonators?'

'Oh, yes, I think so.'

'They are linked to a network of neutrino-bombs buried in the ice fields,' Ishka continued. 'We are engineers forced to work on their development of neutrino-boosted nuclear divisive energy – the two most powerful forces in nature.'

'But won't that destroy everything?'

Ishka pulled at his beard. 'I would have thought so. But those green devils must plan to survive. Do you know how, Peri?'

'I heard them say something about the next hour being vital for detonation.'

'The Ice Warriors must have a plan for their own survival, but they won't care about ours.'

'Can you not escape into the underways through the ice?' Peri asked.

The Salvakians looked at her.

'Some of us have tried,' Hussa said quietly.

'What happened?'

'Scythed down. Including Sira. They must have kept her clothing.'

Peri remembered the scorch mark in the back of the tunic she was wearing.

'I'm sorry, I didn't know.'

'She would want you to use it.' Ishka wiped an eye and turned away overcome at the memory. Peri wandered to the doorway.

Instantly Farn hissed ominously from outside, 'You will stay inside!'

'Just wondered when the hot drinks trolley was due

to arrive,' Peri said with a lightness she was far from feeling.

'Go back or you will die!' the monster rasped back at her.

Peri understood and retreated back into the igloo. Ishka had regained his composure. 'Have you no friends, companions?' he questioned.

It was Peri's turn to feel the pain of loss. 'I don't know what happened to them. They must have been crushed, destroyed by those monsters.' After this Peri felt hope ebb away from them all.

Sensing her despair, Ishka said gently, 'Then there is no chance of rescue.' He led Peri gently towards a fur pelt rug where they all settled into a huddle for warmth. 'Tell us of your strange world of Magnus, Peri, during these last minutes before the Ice Warriors destroy it for ever.'

'That isn't going to be easy,' Peri began, but was interrupted by movement outside. Crawling towards the entrance they heard two Ice Warriors speaking in their husky voices.

'Have you seen other humans near?'

'No.'

'Keep close watch!'

Inside the cell of ice blocks the group looked at each other. 'My friends,' Peri whispered. 'They must have survived.' Her spirits revived. She listened intently to sounds outside, hearing the heavy crunching footsteps of Craag leave. Then there was only the hissing breath of Farn, the sentry posted to prevent their escape. Suddenly she heard the Warrior move and give an exclamation of alarm. She took a chance and peeped out of the entrance in time to see the Doctor and Vion facing the outstretched weapon arm of the Ice Warrior, Farn. Peri hurled herself at the giant leg before her. Her impact was small but the surprise attack caused the beam of force to go off target, smashing into the ceiling above.

'Run!' Peri shouted to the Salvakians who had emerged from the cell. They all began running away from the irate Ice Warrior, who had regained his balance and was preparing to fire again. Zig-zagging and running towards the Doctor and Vion they were assisted by a sudden fall of ice that partly blocked the space between Farn and themselves.

'Quickly!' the Doctor called to the Salvakians as Peri joined him. From the fallen mound of ice they could hear the Ice Warrior blasting his way through towards them.

'Detonators . . . we must disarm,' Ishka panted.

'No time,' the Doctor said. 'Down here!'

Farn had now smashed his way through the barrier of ice and was clumping towards them, weapon arm ready to fire. Using their advantage of speed the group charged towards a corner that would give them temporary safety. Half a dozen paces short of this sanctuary Rodan slipped on the treacherous surface. Ishka turned to help his companion but already Farn was pointing the sonic weapon towards them.

'No!' the Doctor shouted and pulled Ishka out of the line of fire. Rodan regained his feet but was too late. Exposed, he presented an easy target, and the blast of sonic power devastated him. The force of impact made his body vibrate for a second before falling, a lifeless doll, features twisted by the shock of death.

Horrified at the destruction, the group stood transfixed. Vion was the first to sense the danger. 'Let's go!' he shouted. 'He is dead. We're not. Move quickly, everyone!' They wrenched their attention from the horror of Rodan's death and saw the Ice Warrior thudding towards them. Without another word they turned and ran for their lives.

11

With some distance gained Ishka recognized a particular formation in an ice cave. 'Wait. We are near to Vedikael's main control chamber.'

'Who?' the Doctor paused. Panting, the others gathered about them, their breath steaming in the chilled air.

'Vedikael, the commander of the Ice Warriors.'

'Ah, yes?' the Doctor made an effort to recall. 'Marshal, Grand Marshal? Is the Grand Marshal here?' he asked.

The Salvakian leader shook his head. 'We were hardly allowed into the main control chamber. We were slave labour, clearing tunnels of ice falls.'

'Perhaps we should take a look at their operations room?' the Doctor said.

'Shouldn't we find a detonator and disarm it?' Ishka asked.

'No time.' The decisive tone of the Doctor persuaded Ishka of the urgency of their situation. They moved quietly through the passage gouged from the ice towards a much larger chamber which had been hollowed out by the Ice Warriors. The entrance was unguarded, just a crude opening wide enough to allow the bulk of the giant aliens through.

Just as they were about to advance further they were alerted by a heavy tread from the opposite passage. Shrinking back out of sight the Doctor and his companions remained unseen as Craag and Farn went lumbering into the control chamber.

'What is being planned in there?' the Doctor whispered to Ishka.

'A massive explosion: accelerated nuclear blast.'

'To what end?'

'That we do not understand.'

'Then we'd better find out.'

'How?'

'Let's take a look.' The Doctor edged his way along the cold walls until he reached the opening to the chamber. Hesitantly the others followed his lead.

Inside the chamber, eight Ice Warriors were attending to a control centre that linked the detonators to the neutrino bombs. Each concentrated fully on the synchronometer that was counting down to a red zone marked 'Detonation'. Vedikael, smaller and more agile than his warriors, patrolled between the monitors tensely, then paused to check a VDU for a conjunction of orbital planetary positions.

The setting was an eerie one, with the green, reptilian aliens standing out starkly against the cold blue of the ice chamber walls. The technological equipment they were intent on manipulating gave a surreal quality to these prehistoric monsters who were about to alter the future of an entire planet.

Having seen the site of the Ice Warriors power base the Doctor returned to the others and began to issue instructions. 'Vion, that force stick: give it to me.'

'It's no good, the armour of the Ice Warriors is too strong.'

'But the ice isn't,' the Doctor replied, directing a beam of energy against the outer chamber wall. Slowly the ice began to melt. 'We must divert their attention, make an attempt to damage their ignition circuitry, to gain time somehow.' The Doctor passed the force stick to Ishka. 'Follow the wall twenty paces along. That should bring you to a spot that lies behind the first monitor. Use the force stick to break through, then destroy as much of their technology as you can. I'll divert them as long as I'm able. We may be destroyed but at least a world might be saved.'

'Doctor . . .' Peri started, but with a slight smile the Doctor patted her shoulder then sauntered towards the entrance to the Ice Warriors's chamber. They watched him disappear inside without a pause.

The Doctor's appearance was instantly noticed. He tried to remain composed while eight weapon arms swung towards him. Vedikael moved across the chamber to confront the intruder. 'Who are you?' The strange glowing eyes surveyed the motley figure. Angry red orbs stared into impish blue eyes.

'I am the Doctor.'

'What is it you want?'

The guttural speech grated on the Doctor's ears but he forced himself to be flippant, hoping that by now the force stick would be carving into the ice, allowing an attack – if not a rescue. 'I thought I'd pop in and see what you warrior chaps were keeping on ice.' The Doctor smiled blandly.

'No strangers are allowed here. Kill him!' The incensed Vedikael raised his arm to signal execution.

'Come, come, don't you Ice Lords learn anything at all?' said the Doctor rapidly. 'Look at you, pathetic survivors of a once great Martian race!'

The arm of Vedikael remained raised. 'We will be magnificent once more, with this new planet as our home. Soon this world will be made perfect for breeding and hatching. Then our race will rise again from the ashes of Magnus!' Croaking noises of excitement supporting Vedikael came from the assembled Ice Warriors. Beyond them the Doctor noticed an opening beginning to grow in the wall of the ice chamber behind the monitoring units.

'How can a race as stupid as you accomplish anything?' The Doctor sauntered to a display screen and glanced at it. 'Nuclear based bombs. How unsubtle.'

'That is enough, Doctor ... Doctor?' Vedikael paused as the Doctor saw Ishka's head emerge from the opening in the wall of ice. 'Doctor?' Vedikael's eyes glowed with hatred. 'You have thwarted the Grand Marshal's plans more than once before, have you not?'

'Yes, that's right.'

'Hold your fire.' Vedikael spoke to his warriors and stared at the Doctor. 'I, Vedikael, will deliver you to the feet of his eminence. When the great one descends, you will be sacrificed in his honour.'

Stealthily, Ishka, Peri, Vion and the other two Salvakians entered the chamber. The Doctor smiled up into the arrogant features of the Martian. 'I'm afraid sacrifice doesn't appeal overmuch, sorry . . .' He broke off as the group led by Ishka launched themselves at the countdown monitors. Bellowing with rage the Ice Warriors turned to repel the intruders. A mêlée developed with the Doctor and his comrades bravely trying to damage and delay the countdown to nuclear desctruction, dodging around the clumsy warriors. The great strength of the creatures was too much, however. Flinging himself out of Jarga's path, the Doctor yelled, 'Retreat, Ishka, retreat. Get out while you still can!'

A wave of sonic force fired by Skaag destroyed Hussa as he struck at a VDU panel showing details of planetary conjunction. The Doctor shouted once more to Ishka as he evaded a lunge from Jarga, 'Get out! Everyone!' Dodging the clumsy attempts to stop them, the crestfallen group retreated with the Ice Warriors starting in ponderous pursuit.

'Come back!' the voice of their commander stopped his warriors in their tracks. 'You must all assist in here! Repair any damage. Holocaust detonation is imminent – we must not miss this time! Repair that first!' Vedikael pointed to the monitor that Hussa had damaged. It crackled with static and the flashes of power discharge as two warriors began repairs.

* * *

When the Doctor and his companions realized that there was no pursuit they slowed and halted, panting for breath. Their mood was one of despair. The Doctor tried to think of something to raise their spirits. 'Let us return to the detonator we discovered. We will disarm that.' It was not much to offer but any action was preferable to being slumped against a wall of ice contemplating imminent annihilation.

Wearily the group begin to move away from the chamber where the Ice Warriors were about to bring their plan to its final solution.

12

Sil waved his short arms at the women who surrounded him accusingly. 'I simply . . .'

'Yes, yes, you keep gurgling on about it,' Jarmaya said acidly, cutting short Sil's protestations.

'What exactly did you do, Sil? Try to remember.' Zandusia spoke calmly.

'I went . . .' Sil hesitated, staring at the knobs, switches, levers and buttons on the TARDIS control panel before him. 'Yes, I . . .' he paused again in confusion. 'No, I . . .' With some bravado he pressed a lever, turned a handle, depressed a switch. Nothing happened. 'No, perhaps . . . As he reached to try again Jarmaya lost patience and went to remove him bodily from his position at the control panel. Panicking, Sil grabbed a pair of levers and clung on terrified at Jarmaya's anger. As Jarmaya pulled Sil away the driving column lifted and fell.

'Stop!' the Rana yelled.

'There, there, I've done it!' Sil squealed. 'These two

levers, these. Now we can return!' Released from Jarmaya's grip he was about to pull the levers again when Zandusia restrained him.

'No. No. We will not return. I feel the danger is so great that we must remain in time ahead of the disaster.'

'But Rana,' Jarmaya said.

'It is too late to avert the destruction. At least this way we will save our lives.'

'Are they worth saving?' Jarmaya gestured at the grim scene of destruction shown on the screen.

'That is my decision,' said the Rana. 'We stay here for a further hour.'

The sounds of the ice became more and more ominous, groaning and cracking above the Doctor and his party. It was as if the planet of Magnus itself was apprehensive at the forces about to be unleashed upon it.

'Wait.' Ishka pointed to a widening split in the roof and a powdering of ice descending ahead of them. 'Let's try to get through,' he urged.

They began to move with alacrity towards the dangerous section. Before they could reach it the dome of the passage ahead disintegrated, bringing down an avalanche of ice that completely sealed the corridor ahead. Angrily Vion began to dig at the ice.

'No, Vion.' The Doctor pulled the boy away from the hopeless attempt.

'What can we do?' Peri asked hopelessly. 'Their bombs must be due to explode any minute. We're going to die, and without even knowing why.'

'The Ice Warriors have their own mad logic . . .' the Doctor started, then staggered and slapped his forehead. 'At last! Yes, at last I understand!'

The others looked at each other in puzzlement while the Doctor grabbed the force stick from Ishka's belt and with grim determination gave his orders. 'All of you, find a space, dig in, hide there. I must try to prevent the detonation at any cost!'

'Doctor!' Ishka began but the Doctor had turned and was running at great speed back towards the cave of the Ice Warriors. Ishka looked at Peri.

'He has gone to attack the Ice Warriors single-handedly. But why take the force stick? It was spent in breaking through that chamber wall!'

When the Doctor reached the control chamber he found the Ice Warriors busily intent on the final phase of the thermonuclear experiment conceived by the evil brain of their Grand Marshal. The Doctor saw a chronometer showing one minute to ignition, fifty nine seconds, fifty eight . . .

'Stop, wait, hold!' The Doctor levelled the force stick at the nearest monitor.

'Put away your puny toy, Doctor,' Vedikael grated as he and the other Ice Warriors turned to face the Doctor. 'Put that stick away, Doctor, it cannot harm us.'

'No, but it can disrupt!' The Doctor pressed the control button, but no wave of force came from the empty weapon. He hurled the stick at the nearest monitor, but it bounced harmlessly down onto the soiled ice of the chamber floor.

'Now who is pathetic, Doctor?' Vedikael sneered and turned to Skaag. 'Cover him. If he moves, kill!'

'Commander,' Skaag acknowledged and pointed the weapon on his arm forward with deadly intent. Helplessly the Time Lord saw the figures of the chronometer dip below five seconds, then four, three, two, one . . . and the world of Magnus seemed to reverse on its axis. A shock wave of shuddering intensity swept through the underground chamber. The Doctor was hurled against a wall. Even the Ice Warriors, with their far greater strength, stumbled and swayed and lost their bearings in the holocaust that their neutrino bombs had unleashed.

A second wave struck with such force that even the Ice Warriors could not maintain their balance. One by one they toppled to the floor. The turmoil in the chamber, the shuddering of the walls and the frequent falls of ice gave the Doctor the chance to crawl away unnoticed by his captors. His last view of the control chamber was one of pandemonium, with dazed and fallen Ice Warriors stumbling around in confusion. Only Commander Vedikael seemed unaffected. The Martian War Lord raised his arms in triumph.

'At last we conquer. At last our race has a home. Now we can arise and conquer!'

The Doctor crawled slowly along a passage whose walls were narrowed by icefalls but still just passable.

'Doctor!' a familiar voice called to him from behind.

'Peri?' The Doctor saw his companion with Vion, Ishka and Dabasir. Like the Doctor they looked shocked and surprised to have survived the holocaust unleashed by the Ice Warriors. A gale of wind hit them, followed by further gusts which forced them to the ground. There they lay pinned by the pull of powerful gravitational forces. It was as if the world of Magnus had been torn from its normal orbit.

The Doctor tried to raise himself and found the G-forces had eased their grip. Then the howling icy wind lessened its force a little. If it was like this under-ground, what of the peoples and cities above? The Doctor regained his feet and tried to help Peri up. His companion was looking as sickly as a victim of sea sickness.

'Wh-what's happened, Doctor?' she asked faintly.

'It's the Ice Warriors,' the Doctor replied. 'They wanted to change the climate of Magnus by altering the orbit of the planet. That explosion was timed to fling Magnus further from its sun. The temperature will go down – it'll be almost perpetual winter. Ideal for the Ice Warriors but desperate for everyone else.'

'These are the revelations, Doctor?' asked Vion, who had been helped to his feet by Ishka and Dabasir.

'In a way. Come on, we must leave this ice warren before it caves in and we are buried alive.'

Battling against the onrushing wind and with many a fearful glance at the groaning dome of ice above, they began their retreat south.

13

Order had been restored in the chamber of the Ice Warriors. Vedikael and his troops were standing to attention before a screen that showed the Grand Marshal addressing them with some approval at the success of their mission.

'You have succeeded admirably. Our sightings and readings show an orbital tilt axial adjustment of 3.4 degrees, which we calculate will cause a climatic change entirely in our favour.' A grimace that was the way the Grand Marshal expressed pleasure briefly contorted his speckled features. 'You may prepare this world for my coming.'

'Yes, Grand Marshal!' Vedikael and the rest of the Ice Warriors saluted in unison, fists slamming into shoulders, confirming their fanatical commitment to the will of their leader.

Creaking and rumbling, the corridors of ice became more and more threatening to the Doctor and his companions as they travelled back in the direction they hoped would lead to the rockways and away from the constant danger of being engulfed by the collapse of the ice tunnels.

'Are you sure this is the right way, Vion?' Peri gasped.

'I've lived underground all my life. You develop an instinct.'

'I hope it's working,' Peri muttered to herself as they slogged on through the deathly cold, all the while trying to avoid the chunks of ice that occasionally slammed down from above.

The medium Ulema had been searching for the Rana and her court when the chaos of the orbital adjustment had occurred. Now she was lost, wandering the rockways in the hope of contacting someone – anyone. She paused, held a forefinger to either side of her temples and sent a mind scan ahead. There was something: something or someone ahead, faint but positive. She set off in the direction of the source of contact.

Eventually she found herself in a darkened passage. Lighting her torch rod she shone the beam ahead of her and saw with surprise that the passage was blocked by a fall of snow and ice. Puzzled, she approached the barrier, tested it and confirmed that here the rock finished and the ice began.

At the same moment, only feet away on the other side of the ice fall, the Doctor, Peri, Ishka and Dabasir stood watching Vion close his eyes and carefully place a forefinger to each temple.

'I'm sure the rockways start just beyond here,' Vion said. 'There's something, someone . . .'

'How can you know?' Peri asked, unimpressed.

'Peri . . .' the Doctor admonished.

'Listen, Peri,' Vion rejoined. 'I'm telling you, after this ice there's the rockways and some safety!'

'You're guessing.' Peri said crossly. She was cold, hungry and disliked Vion's manner of male self-importance. 'Typical man,' she added.

'She *is* from Magnus,' Ishka said. 'I'd heard their women were crosspatches.'

'Can we do something other than talk?' Peri stamped her foot, then realized how numb it was with cold.

'Do stop bickering, Vion, and try your mind scan again,' the Doctor said. A trifle self-consciously, the young man closed his eyes, adjusted fingers to temples and lapsed into concentrated silence.

On the other side of the blocked passageway, Ulema was in a similar attitude to Vion. Suddenly her eyes opened in panic at the mind she had located only yards away. Crouching down she took a force stick from her belt, and pointed it at the ice mound. She was determined to destroy as many invaders as she could.

'Dig!' said Vion, leading by example and attacking the ice with his bare hands.

'Yes!' Ishka said, clambering up to help the boy. Soon the others joined him, and the ice began to fly as they burrowed from up near the roof where, if they were lucky, the blockage was thinner.

Ulema could hear the male voices, could see the ice beginning to crumble and fall from near the roof. She switched off her light rod and waited in the darkness with her force stick set to inflict maxiumum damage.

'I'm through!' Vion shouted. 'Help me!'

The others scrambled to enlarge the opening at the top of the ice mound. Soon it was large enough for Ishka to peer through.

'Darkness. I can't . . .'

'Let me look.' Vion stared into the gloom beyond. 'It is the rock tunnel. I'll lead us through.' As he spoke, the boy pulled himself through and disappeared from view.

'It's all right!' they heard him call. One by one they followed his lead, with Peri the last to slide down the slope. It was fortunate that she was a little behind the rest. Ulema, thinking the group was complete, switched on her rod of light and was about to blast the four surprised men when Peri came sliding down the ice slope and cannonned into the medium, causing her to drop the force stick. Peri and Ulema began to struggle for possession of the fallen weapon.

'Let me go!' Ulema cried. 'They are from Salvak. I must kill them, it is my duty!' The struggle was resolved by Ishka seizing the force stick and training it on Ulema with every intention of blasting the Magnusian woman.

'No!' the Doctor roared. 'She is our way into the

mind of Magnus. Kill her and we have no hope of reconciling the women and uniting against the Ice Warriors!'

In answer to this Ulema launched herself at Ishka, who staggered under the attack of the wildcat. Holding the kicking and scratching girl at arms length he spoke with loathing, 'Are they all like this down here?'

'She's one of the quieter ones. Bit of an intellectual, I'd say,' the Doctor said.

'No wonder the Ice Warriors wanted to destroy these she-devils!' Ishka shook the girl again.

'*You* are the destroyers!' Ulema spat back at him, eyes hot with rage and hatred.

The Doctor placed himself between the woman of Magnus and the man from Salvak. 'Listen to me, Ulema, listen! You may enter my mind to find the truth of what has befallen your world. You may examine my thoughts for the truth of our intentions.' Warily the medium quietened then nodded. The others watched as Ulema and the Time Lord went into each other's minds. They stood no more than a foot apart with their eyes closed.

'What sorcery is this?' Ishka muttered to Dabasir.

'Like minds attract,' Peri said dryly. 'They are each as crazy as the other.'

Ulema began to speak in a low voice, swaying slightly before the Doctor. 'Your thoughts confuse and frighten me, Doctor.'

'I know exactly how she feels,' Peri said to Vion, watching the Doctor and Ulema beginning to emerge from their psychic contact. The Doctor opened his eyes then after some seconds, Ulema did the same.

'Now you know the truth of what I have seen, and you know of the Ice Warriors.' Ulema nodded. 'What I do not know,' the Doctor continued, 'is what has befallen my TARDIS. Has it been requisitioned, cannibalized, dissected, destroyed?'

Ulema sighed. 'I do not know. I have lost contact with my sisters. I do not understand why. I was searching for the Rana. I had gone underground to ask the Matrons, when the world shifted, there was a rushing wind, falling buildings, fire in the heavens, death, destruction and the Rana, Jarmaya, all the Court, gone.' Her long dark hair fell forward as her head bowed in sadness. She was unrecognizable now as the tigress of only five minutes earlier. Peri stepped forward on impulse to comfort her.

'She's crying,' Vion said in wonder to the Doctor.

'Yes. It helps at times. Come on Ulema, you can weep as we go along. Lead on, Vion. Guide us back to where I left my TARDIS.'

'I'll try, Doctor,' Vion said, lighting the rod and walking into the rockways, leaving the tunnel of ice behind them.

The screen in the TARDIS explored the fallen walls of the winter palace of Rana Zandusia. With Jarmaya at the controls the screen showed the extent of the damage to be less extensive than at first sight, but to those who knew and had loved the palace the view was heartbreaking. Dust and the grey overcast atmosphere settled on what appeared to be a haunted ruin rather than a vibrant centre of power and government.

The Rana turned away. 'Stop it. I cannot bear to look any more.'

'Wait a moment!' Sil exclaimed. 'Something moved. There!' Jarmaya moved in and enlarged the picture.

The massive head of an Ice Warrior filled the screen of the TARDIS. The women shrank away. 'What devil is that – a Salvakian?' a courtier voiced her fear.

'What else can it be.' The Rana assumed control. 'We must return. We must fight these Salvakian monsters!'

Sil giggled. The Rana frowned angrily. 'I see nothing to cause amusement, Sil.'

'Nervousness, I do assure you,' said Sil, controlling his delight at seeing Ice Warriors making themselves at home on Magnus.

'Synchronise the return time!' Zandusia ordered. 'I wish to join my people. I would rather die fighting those monsters than live in this limbo of safety.'

Jarmaya began to make the adjustments to the co-ordinates that she hoped would return them to the present.

'It was here you first emerged, Doctor. The caves of the Magnii.' Vion indicated the empty cavern.

The Doctor stared at the space where his TARDIS had been. Quietly he spoke to Ulema. 'Where might they take it?' The medium went into a mind scan then shook her head. 'Nothing. There is no message, no reflection of its energy, nothing.'

'Almost as if it had never existed,' the Doctor said thoughtfully.

'That would mean *we* had never existed. Talk sense, Doctor,' said Peri.

'No, Peri. If the Sisters of Science or whatever they call themselves have been daft enough to tamper with the TARDIS they could have triggered a time safety jump and been catapulted into the future. They'll be waiting for our time wave to catch them up.'

'How long into the future?'

'The TARDIS has a different view of eternity to you or even I. What it thought of as a safety margin could be five minutes or even five hundred years.'

'We could be here on Magnus for *five hundred* years?'

'Yes.' The Doctor began to settle himself on a nearby rock. 'May as well make ourselves comfy, don't you think?'

14

The image of the Grand Marshal came into focus on the communications unit in the chamber of the Ice Warriors. 'You have done well.'

The assembled group hissed with pleasure. Vedikael bowed his acknowledgement of the rare compliment. 'We are ready with the second phase: the bombs are primed and ready.'

'That will not be necessary. Magnus has been propelled into perpetual winter.'

The Ice Warriors wheezed with delight as the Grand Marshal continued. 'Scans around the planet confirm social breakdown, famine, cold, but enough native labour will survive to serve us.'

'And the radiation factor? Did the neutrino fusion produce the safety effect we hoped for?'

'Completely. The dust that now surrounds Magnus is safe and sufficient to keep the weakened rays of the sun from heating the surface.'

'That is wonderful news, Grand Marshal.'

'When my I descend?'

Vedikael considered. His gaze fell upon the large sonic burner being readied for use. 'Very soon I must re-open the tunnels and capture survivors. We have patrols out now.'

'That is unnecessary. Clear the tunnels by all means, but we have enough for our army of slaves. Destroy the rest!'

'Yes, Grand Marshal!'

'Inform me when this is done.'

The screen went blank. Vedikael turned to Skaag. 'Have the ice searing equipment activated. Force its flame down every tunnel.'

'The patrols?'

'Recall them. Then burn everything that moves!'

Everyone in the TARDIS waited for something to happen in response to Jarmaya's manipulation of the console controls. But nothing happened.

'Stupid oafess!' squealed Sil.

Annoyed at the failure, Jarmaya turned angrily. 'Listen, you slime . . .'

'Look!' Zandusia pointed at the driving column which rose and fell, then became inert again.

'I could have become rich during these missing hours,' Sil grumbled, but stopped as the TARDIS dematerialized and the image on the viewing screen began to dissolve.

In the cave of the Magnii the Doctor and the others of his group sat gloomily about. Peri, finding the floor of the cavern rather unyielding, shifted and stared at something that she thought was moving in the shadows. 'Doctor . . .'

'Find a softer rock, Peri. Stop complaining.'

'I thought I saw something move over there.'

'Where?'

Everyone peered in the direction of Peri's pointing finger. Then Peri and the Doctor heard a familiar sound – the sound of materialization! Soon a familiar blue shape appeared. Excitedly Vion and Peri hurried to the old police box. The door opened and Zandusia and Jarmaya stepped from the TARDIS.

'Rana!' Ulema, overjoyed, ran towards the women while Vion backed away in fear.

'You are safe!' Ulema greeted Zandusia.

'Yes, but Magnus isn't. Has our world been destroyed, Ulema?'

'Yes.'

'An explosion?'

The Doctor stepped forward. 'Of massive proportions.'

'Caused by the men of Salvak!'

Zandusia glared with malice at Ishka and Dabasir.

'No.' Ishka stared boldly back at the Rana.

'Who is this?' Rana demanded.

'I am from Salvak.' There was a pause; the half a dozen women examined the two men from Salvak with curiosity and expressions of contempt and loathing.

'Don't blame them, they are innocent,' the Doctor interrupted the staring contest. 'Your world has been attacked by Ice Warriors under the control of their Grand Marshal.'

'For what purpose? Ice Warriors, why?' Zandusia asked.

The Doctor looked around the assembled throng. 'I believe their object was not simply destruction but to change the orbit of Magnus – to cause its axis to wobble. Your planet is at one of its solstices, I would guess . . .'

'That's right,' Jarmaya said apprehensively.

The Doctor now had everyone's attention. 'I believe the nuclear explosion has forced Magnus into a new orbit of maximum ellipse, maybe doubling its distance from your sun.'

'So our summer would be, what, shorter?' Jarmaya questioned the Doctor.

'Very. Hardly time for the winter snows to thaw.'

Peri shivered at the thought. 'Almost perpetual winter!'

'Yes, Peri, perfect weather for Ice Warriors.'

Peri remembered something she learned at High School. 'The Ice Ages. Milankovitchian cycles . . .?'

Zandusia interrupted with impatience. 'So we are either to be destroyed by Ice Warriors or the winter they have created?'

Sil clapped his hands for attention. 'I can help with the weather. I have bought a great number of winter woollies and stored them safely underground. I should make a cosy killing now, don't you think?' Sil could no longer contain his delight. His cackling laugh burst forth with demonic intensity, filling the cave with its discordancy.

* * *

The Ice Warriors Jarga and Farn were exploring the rockways nearby when they heard the sound of Sil's mad laughter. Pausing only to set their weapons in readiness they began to advance menacingly towards the site of the maniacal outburst.

'Be quiet!' Jarmaya's scream of rage finally quelled the Thoros Betan's mirth.

'How is it,' the Rana asked Sil ominously, 'that you alone had the foresight to prepare for such a happening?'

'Luck, my lady. Who can grow rich without it?' The laughter gurgled in Sil's throat uncontrollably then died as Sil saw a green armoured carapace, a levelled arm, the glowing tip of a sonic weapon. 'No!' he managed to croak before a force bolt shimmered towards him. 'Ah!' he squealed, ducking down into his water tank. The sonic shock wave swept over the group, devastating Sil's attendants and a screaming courtier.

The women scattered, yelling and crying out in panic. The Ice Warriors prepared to fire again. Caught in the rush Peri stumbled, tried to hold her balance, then fell to her knees in the path of the advancing warriors.

'Peri!' The Doctor came back for her and tried to raise her quickly but it was too late. Farn levelled his gun at Peri and prepared to fire. Fortunately his last order had been to guard her, and the slight confusion in the giant biped's mind saved her life. Farn gestured with his gun, and Peri and the Doctor shrank back against a wall.

Hauling himself up in his tank, Sil called across to Farn and Jarga. 'I am Sil!'

Farn turned, hissing out, 'Who?'

Jarga intervened. 'He is to assist us. Let him live.' The Doctor smiled and moved into the cave along with the watchful Ice Warriors and Peri.

'Ah, good old Sil, backing both ends against everyone else as usual.'

Sil chortled. 'First rule of business – always side with the winning side. Something you have a marked tendency not to do, Doctor!'

'Enough talk,' Jarga said. 'Orders are to kill all we find.'

Farn, happy now that the matter had been made clear, raised his sonic energy weapon and prepared to execute the Doctor and Peri. Sil clapped delightedly. 'Fare thee well, Doctor. No profit in allowing you to live!' Peri and the Doctor exchanged last glances. What a way to die, with the jarring laughter of Sil sounding in their ears. Then his hilarity ceased abruptly. 'Aargh! Wait. Stop. Cease execution!'

Surprised, the Ice Warriors turned to Sil. 'Where is Lord Vedikael?' Sil demanded.

'I believe he was last at Ice Station Control.'

'I must join him, and as you have slain my carrying maidens the Doctor and this revolting creature must carry me!'

'Who, me?' Peri asked.

'Who else?' Sil gloated. 'Are there any other creatures here more revolting?'

'Creature? *You'd* be barred from a cockroach convention!'

'Don't talk to Sil like that, Peri,' the Doctor said mildly. 'Show some respect.'

'Yes, listen to the Doctor, you ugly piece of wenchhood.'

'No point wasting time,' the Doctor said, crossing and making ready to lift the carrying poles attached to Sil's water tank.

'Wait!' Sil said, suspecting a ruse.

'Yes?'

'Give her the heavy end to carry.'

'Good idea,' the Doctor agreed.

'What? I won't do it!'

'Stop arguing, Peri, I would welcome a chance to visit Lord Vedikael at his Ice Station, I really would.'

Although she suspected the Doctor was planning a desperate throw, her pride was difficult to overcome. Then Jarga thrust her roughly towards the Thoros Betan. 'The heavy end, right,' said Peri and bent to take a pole in each hand. With the Doctor leading they began to trundle away. Carrying the tank was not easy and Sil swayed from side to side as they tried to adjust their rhythm.

'Steady, steady! No spillage or you will not be allowed to bathe my pretty-pretty personage later!' Sil turned to regard the sullen Peri. 'Why is she not smiling over her lot, Doctor?'

Trudging along with an Ice Warrior clumping ahead and another behind him the Doctor still tried to keep up a little banter. 'Peri has no concept of what it really means to be your body servant, Sil.'

'She must learn – and quickly. I order you to learn

to smile while doing the honour of carrying my person.'

'I'll try, frog, toad.'

'Lower order of Savria?' the Doctor suggested.

'Oh, yes!'

'Enough of this flattery,' Sil said, 'you slackers!' The Thoros Betan began to urge his carriers on by bouncing forward on his perch.

'Quickly, quickly, I must meet with Lord Vedikael soon!'

Outside the boys' dormitory, Rana Zandusia and the survivors had gathered for a conference. Unfortunately this had quickly degenerated into a heated exchange of opinion between her and Ishka, while a dozen wide-eyed boys watched in amazement as a male dared to treat a woman as an equal.

'I must return to my palace. Only from there can I communicate with my people. I am Rana here!'

'Your people are no more, your power is no more. You are reacting like any woman, with panic and hysteria.'

'You'd know, would you? What woman could you possibly know who would speak to you?'

'I am ruler of Avata, a continent of Salvak, Avatarian women react just like you.'

'Like what?'

'Like a silly Woltrop bird who squawks orders to the breeze without thought, reason or understanding!'

Listening to this row made Vion chortle. Jarmaya glared at him before turning her scorn towards the two men from Salvak. 'How dare you address the

Rana in such terms!' Jarmaya unsheathed her ring; Zandusia smiled.

'Take them to savour the air above. Let's see if their male insolence survives exposure to our Magnusian sunshine.'

Ishka snorted in derision. 'Madam, you need a . . .' Ishka started forward but a force beam quickly enveloped him. He was halted in mid-stride – temporarily frozen and inanimate. Dabasir tried to retreat, but received similar treatment from Jarmaya.

Zandusia turned to a matron. 'Take these males up to the surface. Leave them so that the sun may warm their blood thoroughly.'

'Did you say sun, Rana?'

'I did.'

'There is no sun. Not any more.' Then she stopped, shocked at the appearance of a group of Ice Warriors. Jandaan, second in command to Vedikael, stepped forward arrogantly.

'Which of you is called the Rana?' he rasped.

'I am.'

'You are under arrest by order of the Grand Marshal!'

In the control chamber of the Ice Station, Skaag and Gorga were bent over the controls of the sonic ice burner. Left in charge by Vedikael, Skaag could not manage to engage the firing mechanism with his clumsy fingers. 'Always those Salvakians helped us with this,' he said, fumbling and failing once again. A noise made him look up as Sil, supported by the

111

Doctor and Peri, bounced in, accompanied by Farn and Jarga.

Relieved at the sight of the more dexterous Jarga, Skaag pointed at the ice burner. 'You must ignite, Jarga, Lord Vedikael's order is that we clear all ice tunnels!'

'It will be done.' Jarga saluted as Skaag examined Sil.

'What is this?'

'My name is Sil. I prepared the way for your conquest in return for certain business considerations.'

'I know nothing of this.'

'Lord Vedikael . . .' Sil started.

'Said nothing of you. Presumably you had served your purpose.'

Sil did not find the brusque attitude endearing. 'I demand to see the Grand Marshal!' he screamed. 'I insist on an audience!'

'No,' Skaag's voice grated with finality.

'Lord Vedikael . . . where is he?' Sil faltered.

'Gone to the palace. Rana Zandusia has been captured.'

In the ensuing pause Skaag became aware that the Doctor had quietly drifted to the long cylindrical silvered metal ice burner and was glancing down at the fuel propulsion ignition unit. 'What are you doing?' hissed Skaag.

'Wondering why you cannot get this to work,' the Doctor said cheerfully. 'All you need do is this and this.' He pressed two tiny switches and depressed a lighted panel. With a roar the sonic burner blazed into life.

'Stop!' Skaag stormed.

'Sorry!' The Doctor switched the device off and held his hands up in innocence.

Skaag considered. He was worried about failing to carry out the orders of Lord Vedikael. He turned to Jarga, 'Use the ice burner at once.' He turned to salute another four Ice Warriors as they marched into the cave. 'We must prepare to leave the ice station and travel to the palace. There we will make ready for the descent of the Grand Marshal.' All the warriors saluted.

'What of these?' Farn indicated the Doctor, Peri and Sil. The trio saw the massive helmeted head of Skaag turn, then felt the glowing red eyes examine them each in turn.

'The last order I had was that no further slaves are needed. Kill them!'

The Doctor acted instantly. He reached down, rapidly ignited the ice burner and with a yell for Peri to 'Duck!' turned the searing force on to the Ice Warriors as they thudded towards him. Skaag was the first to be caught in the ray of incandescence. With a guttural cry he shimmered and croaked with shock, then slumped to the ground with a heavy crash.

Grimly the Doctor turned the sonic burner on the other warriors. Helpless before the shattering assault, they succumbed to the waves of force. Only Jarga escaped. Backed into a corner he aimed his weapon arm at the Doctor, who struggled to pull the weight of the ice burner around to aim at the last remaining Ice Warrior.

It was Peri who made the decisive move. Scooping water from Sil's tank she threw it at Jarga's vizor. The moment it took for the alien to clear his vision was all the time needed to bring the burner to bear. As Jarga lumbered across the chamber the Doctor released the sonic power for the last time.

The mighty green biped staggered, raised his arm and lurched against Sil's water tank, overturning its terrified occupant. Then he fell face forward onto the floor. The giant lungs fought for one last wheezing breath, then failed. The giant frame shuddered, then became still.

Shaken by the violence, Peri and the Doctor met in the centre of the ice station. There, in the silence, among the fallen Ice Warriors, they became aware not only of the sounds of the machines and communications units, but also a familiar plaintive voice.

'Help!' it said, 'I have not got immersion. Doctor, dear Peri, please!'

The Doctor and Peri looked at each other while Sil thrashed helplessly on the floor of ice. 'Let's be magnanimous,' the Doctor said.

'Must we?'

'Oh, yes.'

Gingerly Peri helped lift Sil back onto his perch while the Doctor placed lumps of ice in Sil's tank to replenish the fluid.

'What now, Doctor?' Peri asked.

'We must find a way to restore the status quo.'

'What is that?' Sil asked suspiciously.

114

'The way things were.'

'Sil's hardly interested in that,' said Peri, observing the scowling features of the Thors Betan.

'I have been betrayed. The Ice Warriors, as you heard, have reneged on my contracts and franchises.'

'Yes, they would do that.' The Doctor was wandering from one unit to another, staring intently at each and scribbling in a notebook.

'No wonder they are not on the inter-galactic business registers,' Sil snarled, then brooded a little more before announcing, 'All deals are off. I wish to be revenged.'

'Oh, how?' Peri asked.

'I know a lot about their plans,' said Sil, darkly.

Across the chamber the Doctor turned from a display screen. 'Many of these units are linked to the ignition circuits of an unused chain of neutrino bombs.'

'Yes, yes. The Ice Warriors kept explosives in reserve in case they needed to manoeuvre the planet further if the first attempt proved unsuccessful.'

The Doctor stared at Sil, then turned back to the display units. After consulting his notebook, he settled himself before a screen showing details of the orbital ellipse of Magnus.

'What is it, Doctor?' Sil asked.

'You may have given me an idea, Sil. Thank you.'

'Oh, really?' Sil preened himself. 'Well, Doctor, Peri, what are friends for but to help each other in times of need?'

Peri shook her head, then smiled. Then she laughed. There was no other way to deal with Sil and the situation. Sil joined in uneasily, but the Doctor paid no attention to them. He was adjusting and co-ordinating the various systems. A chronometer glowed into life above the master detonation unit. It read two minutes to ingition. Then one minute fifty-nine . . .

15

A phalanx of Ice Warriors with Lord Vedikael at their head stood in the courtyard of the palace. With a cruel smile the War Lord watched the Rana and what remained of her court being escorted through the fallen slabs of masonry that littered the courtyard. For the first time the Rana had lost her poise. The damage to her palace, the cold grey swirling mist that filled the courtyard and the menacing ranks of Ice Warriors made Rana Zandusia afraid for the first time in her life. Together with Jarmaya she was thrust before Vedikael.

After a pause the harsh voice sounded on the cold air. 'Soon the Grand Marshal will be here to place his heel to your throats, after which you will, of course, be executed in his honour. Your bodies will be displayed to what remains of your people.'

A distant rumble sounded and the ground began to tremble under their feet. The ranks of Ice Warriors swayed but did not break. Vedikael tried to continue.

'You will . . .'

He was stopped by a massive explosion from the far ice fields that brought everyone to their knees. With the shock of its reverberation the Ice Warriors crawled and struggled to regain their balance as a cyclone hit the palace, smashing into buildings and scattering Ice Warriors and women alike with its primeval force.

At the Ice Station the wind howled on and on with increasing intensity. In the control chamber the Doctor and Peri clung to each other under the grip of the forces exerted by the orbital adjustment.

'Will it work, Doctor?' Sil shouted from nearby.

The Doctor battled against the force of the gale that was swirling within the chamber and pulled himself up against a monitor. It took all his strength to haul himself up to the screen. Once there he peered down at the orbital conjunction. 'I can't tell if we are moving back. I'm not sure if Magnus was still in solstice!'

The wind began to drop. The forces bearing upon them started to lessen as the planet slowed.

'Is Magnus back in its original orbit?'

'I can't say.' The Doctor had just realized that the screen he had been watching was no longer functioning and that the remainder of the instrument panels had also gone dead. The power had failed, probably damaged by the last holocaust.

'Have we succeeded, Doctor?'

The Time Lord sighed. 'I don't know, Peri. Either I've restored the orbit or made a death trap for everyone but the Ice Warriors.'

Peri stared at the Doctor. She realized that for once he was not being flippant – he really did not know whether he had succeeded or failed disastrously. 'Doctor . . .' she started, but was interrupted by the voice of an Ice Warrior that hissed from the doorway.

'You will make yourselves ready to travel with us.'

They saw other warriors outside in the passage and knew that this time there could be no escape.

'Bring them to me!' Vedikael's voice grated harshly as the Ice Warriors regrouped and herded the women who had survived the second holocaust. Vedikael had recovered his certainty as once more the Rana and Jarmaya stood before him. 'Investigations are taking place to decide whether the Grand Marshal should land yet. If you think this means a temporary reprieve I must disappoint you. My orders are to proceed with the extermination of all enemies.'

The Rana saw the two Salvakian men led into the courtyard. Ishka bowed to the Rana who did not know how she should react. She found herself strangely disturbed about the fate of the burly man from Slavak.

'Doctor!' Vedikael turned slowly to greet the Doctor, Peri and Sil, who was perched precariously on the shoulder of an Ice Warrior.

'Lord Vedikael!' Sil called plaintively. 'We had an agreement, a contract.'

Vedikael croaked in derision. 'We are the masters. No agreements need be honoured.'

Sil took in the scene, saw Ice Warriors shepherding

all the survivors to a wall that bounded the palace courtyard. 'What . . . what is to happen here?'

'A little custom we have with conquered races.' Vedikael paused. His voice did not seem to carry as strongly as before, but with an effort he continued. 'You, Sil are not to be trusted: you know far too much. You must, must join the rest for execution.'

Howling his protests Sil was carried away by his Ice Warrior, who deposited him and his tank with the Rana, Jarmaya, Ulema, the two men from Salvak, Vion, Peri and the Doctor. Grimly the group watched the firing squad assemble before them. The squad of twenty Ice Warriors slowly formed a line with Vedikael plodding across to stand at one end, ready to give the signal for the mass execution.

'Why are they taking so long, Doctor?'

'Maybe just spinning it out for their own pleasure.' But now their time had run out. All the Ice Warriors were finally in position.

'Alert,' Vedikael's harsh voice croaked out. Then, after a pause, the Ice Warriors raised their weapons arms. 'Aim,' the War Lord wheezed, panting for breath. Steeling themselves against the sonic blast the condemned waited for a long agonising moment. Then they gazed in astonishment as first one, then another, Ice Warrior crashed to the ground. A ray of sunlight penetrated the grey mist that hung over the palace.

'The heat, the climate: it's returning to its normal temperature!' Peri exulted as warm air, deadly to the Ice Warriors, wreaked havoc upon the giant aliens. One by one they staggered, gasping for breath, before expiring.

Vedikael was the last survivor. 'No surrender,' he gasped as the Rana hurried towards him. He collapsed at her feet, dead.

In the confusion and rejoicing the Doctor came upon Vion, hunched in a corner crying as the sunlight dispelled the last traces of mist. 'What is it, Vion?'

'I don't want to die, Doctor.'

'Why should you?'

'The sunlight . . .'

'Don't worry about that,' Ishka and Dabasir joined them. 'We have an antidote. Enough to protect you until further supplies arrive.'

'Yes,' the Doctor said thoughtfully. 'The frosts of the orbital change may have killed the virus anyway.'

'We will see,' said Ishka as the Rana and Jarmaya arrived.

'See what?'

'How much vaccine to bring in from Salvak, Madam.' Ishka grinned at her.

The Rana frowned. 'You will bring in nothing. We will mobilize. We will fight. We will never submit!'

Ishka stroked his beard. 'How will you fight? With what? Your society is in disarray – it's ruined. You will need our aid to rebuild. I will offer my services now.'

'As what?'

Ishka shrugged, nodded and smiled. 'Isn't it obvious what I would be to you?'

'No, what?'

'A husband.'

Zandusia and Jarmaya glanced at each other blankly. 'What is "husband"?' Zandusia asked.

121

A great laughter came from the two men, then they grinned at the women before them. 'You will learn, ladies!' Ishka said. He and Dabasir guffawed again.

'Ulema!' Rana Zandusia beckoned the medium to her. 'Tell us what this fool has in his mind regarding the word "husband".'

Ulema closed her eyes and then, after some moments, gave a scream of horror. Quickly Jarmaya and the Rana began to comfort her.

'What did you find?' Jarmaya asked. Ulema began to whisper what she had found in the thoughts of the two men from Salvak. 'No!' cried Jarmaya, looking sideways at Dabasir.

'Never!' swore Zandusia, glaring at Ishka.

A furious exchange then broke out between the two couples, watched by Sil who was thinking that Magnus might be a profitable place to invest in matrimonial and baby goods in the near future. He turned to offer the Doctor a partnership, but the Doctor and Peri had decided to leave Magnus to the women and men who would create its future.

A little later the Doctor and Peri stood in the control room of the TARDIS. The Doctor glanced at Peri, who nodded. He touched the flight controls and the driving column began to rise and fall.

In the cave of the Magnii, unobserved by anyone, the old police box faded into the darkness.